REAPER'S WOLVES
MOUNTAIN MC

TIMBER'S GIRL

HALLIE BENNETT

TIMBER'S GIRL

REAPER'S WOLVES MOUNTAIN MC #4

HALLIE BENNETT

Searching for *more* protective heroes? Check out the introduction to Suitor's Crossing and *heart sparks* in the *Mountain Men of Suitor's Crossing* series here[1]!

---

1. https://www.thearrowedheart.com/hallie-bennett

Author's Note

This story features mentions of domestic violence and verbal abuse. There is also on-page violence from an abuser. Please proceed with caution.

Other content notes: On-page sex, cursing, corrupt law enforcement, and family trauma with mention of alcoholism.

Healing after abuse doesn't work on a specific timeline. It could take weeks, months, years before a DV survivor recovers enough for another relationship. In this book, our heroine has done the work of therapy along with choosing to make other healthy decisions. Love in the form of romantic relationships isn't a cure-all for abuse recovery. Please remember this is a work of fiction.

Everyone deserves relationships free from domestic violence. When you're ready, there are people ready to listen with confidential support 24/7/365 at the National Domestic Violence Hotline. Call 800-799-7233 or text BEGIN to 88788.

PROLOGUE

TIMBER

Dog slobber clings to my hand after giving Grim's pitbull, Tiny, a treat from my pocket. I always keep them on hand for him because he's a good boy and deserves it, especially since strangers tend to treat him poorly because of his looks. Something I understand on a visceral level.

Tiny and I? We're two peas in a pod—bulky with muscle and preceded by a bad reputation because of it.

"Hey, are you free? Caroline's friend Lindy, the woman I mentioned in our last club meeting, will be here soon. We'll help move her things into one of the cabins." The president of the Reaper's Wolves MC, Logan Snow, passes us with a raised brow.

"Yeah, I'm heading that way now," I say, continuing down the hall.

When the motorcycle club first relocated to the small mountain town of Suitor's Crossing, this building was an abandoned metal warehouse, an empty shell waiting for us to put our stamp on it. It took a couple of months, but with all of us working together, we converted it into a comfortable clubhouse where most of the MC's members currently reside.

A barn and two log cabins also came with the property, and we quickly added more for families to have privacy—a wise forethought from Snow, since at the time we were all single guys.

He commandeered one for himself when he didn't want to bunk at the clubhouse with the rest of the guys, but I have a feeling the way Snow is acting with his woman means that the cabin situation will become permanent.

The front door creaks open as I step onto the porch where a couple of men are already waiting for our guest.

"You kidnapped my dog again," Grim grumbles, patting his thigh to encourage Tiny to his side rather than mine.

"I can't help it if he likes me better than you."

"It's the bribes. If the vet puts Tiny on a diet, I'm blaming you." Tiny trots down the porch steps to lean against Grim's legs and accept scratches behind his ears.

"Noted." A trail of dust kicks up behind a vehicle turning off the gravel road onto the MC compound. "I think that's our girl."

The SUV slows in front of the clubhouse before continuing down the rocky path to the first cabin—one of seven scattered on the property. It takes a second before the vehicle shuts off as if the woman inside is hesitant about her decision to move onto an MC compound full of men.

Not that I blame her.

Based on Snow's explanation, she's leaving an abusive relationship and needs a safe place to stay.

We probably weren't her first choice, but Caroline, Snow's woman, vouched for us because we're a legit motorcycle club—not a one-percenter dealing with illegal substances or weapons. All of us are military veterans who were looking for brotherhood out of the service, and that's what the Reaper's Wolves MC offers.

The car door swings open, and a riot of red curls are the first thing I notice.

Then the green eyes full of wariness.

And the remnants of a healing bruise on the left side of her neck.

She looks like she's been through hell, and I feel like I just got punched in the gut.

Lindy Thomas is beautiful and brave, and I'm a goner.

Fucking heart sparks...

CHAPTER ONE

PRESENT DAY

LINDY

Y*ou'll always be mine.*

That's what the folded white card says. The printed cursive swirls across the otherwise blank space, and I flip the card over searching for any other clues as to who it's from.

A vase of yellow daisies sat on the welcome mat of my porch this morning. I almost tipped them over in my rush to get out the door and to my standing coffee date with Caroline at Crossing's Cups & Cakes.

Sure, we could chat and drink coffee here at the Reaper's Wolves MC compound, but where's the fun in that? It's nice to hang out in the cute downtown of Suitor's Crossing and enjoy a casual friend date—something I appreciate every damn time after a year of living isolated with my abusive ex.

It's been fourteen months since I left him and moved into the safety of a cabin owned by the MC, but relics of that period in my life still linger in my mind.

Don't think about Dean.

But it's difficult when I read those four words again. *You'll always be mine.* Would Dean be stupid enough to threaten me after all this time? And on a fucking biker compound?

Especially when I know the club has dirt on him. Dirt they won't hesitate to release if he decides to fuck with my life again.

I went through great lengths ensuring my location remained a secret, including smashing my phone to bits so he couldn't track me. Then the fire at Club Wolf happened last week, and Dean—a fucking Everton cop—arrived at the scene.

I know he saw me.

Would he assume because I was with a couple of Reaper's Wolves men that I also lived on their compound?

Seems like a stretch.

Who else would send me flowers and a card, though?

My friends would snicker and point out the obvious suspect. *Timber.* My crazy hot shadow. A tall, bearded military veteran who's appointed himself as my personal protector. But this doesn't seem like his style.

Timber may not say much, but a mysterious gift and note don't strike me as the way he'd declare his interest. Like the rest of the men of the MC, when he wants something or someone, I bet he won't hesitate to claim it. In person. Staring you down with those dark eyes of his.

Groaning, I toss the card aside and grab my purse. I'm already late to meet Caroline. I don't need to stand here fantasizing about Timber's captivating gaze. Or what I'd do if he ever actually decided he wants more than being my security guard.

My track record with men sucks.

And my last boyfriend blew all the other jerks out of the water. Because Dean was an abusive asshole. Physically and mentally. It took all of my strength to leave him, and even then, Caroline had to help me.

Timber is nothing like Dean, but can I risk my heart and well-being again?

No fucking way.

Because I don't think I can survive pain like that a second time around.

CHAPTER TWO

TIMBER

"Timber and Lindy sitting in a tree. K-I-S-S-I-N-G," Fox sings as he enters Reaper's Revamp, the MC's customs auto body shop that I manage. It'd look bad to deck our VP in his smug face, but my fist itches nonetheless.

"You're a fucking menace," I mutter, ignoring the rest of the song about love, marriage, and babies.

"And you're a fucking sap. Yellow daisies? Somehow that's more serious than roses."

"What are you talking about?"

"Come on, don't pretend. Everyone knows you've got a thing for Lindy." Fox looks around the garage, gathering affirmative nods from the other Reaper's Revamp employees and club members. "It's nice to know you're finally doing something about it instead of continuing to lurk around her whenever she makes an appearance."

"I don't lurk," I grumble. Do I make sure I'm within range to protect her if something goes wrong? Sure. But that's not lurking. That's being proactive. Smart. Especially since I've had to step in a couple of times when things got a little dicey with club business.

Like those crazed church congregants who wouldn't leave us alone.

Like the fire at Club Wolf where her ex-boyfriend—*a fucking cop*—showed up at the scene.

"No, you just happen to be Lindy's second shadow." Fox rolls his eyes. "Either way, the yellow daisies were an unexpected move. I didn't peg you as a flower guy."

Tossing my wrench aside, I straighten from my bent position under the hood of a '67 Ford Mustang. It's obvious Fox won't let me work in peace until he's done spouting off whatever nonsense he's going on about.

"Enough with the riddles. What flowers?"

"The ones delivered to Lindy this morning. The prospect on duty signed for them after the driver said who they were for. You didn't send them?"

My gut clenches in tight knots. "No, I didn't."

But I'm going to find out who did.

I've been giving Lindy time to heal after her ordeal with Dean. She's been living on the compound for a while now, and it's no secret how I feel about her. The guys like to tease me about it, and I'm sure Caroline and the rest of her book club friends—which includes Lindy—talk about it, too.

So, who would try to snatch her out from under me by sending a bouquet of flowers?

Fox whistles, his brows lifting in surprise. "Seems your girl's got a secret admirer then, and you've got some competition." He props a booted foot against a red tool cabinet and leans back with his tattooed arms crossed over his chest. "What are you going to do about it? And before you ask... No, Ollie will not hack into the flower shop's records to learn who purchased them."

I figured as much.

But there's no stopping me from questioning the prospect about the bouquet packaging, finding out the shop name, then casually stopping by to do reconnaissance.

CHAPTER THREE

LINDY

Crossing's Cups & Cakes is bustling with customers, making it difficult to find an empty table, but thankfully, a couple leaves right after we grab our drinks from the counter. Hurrying to the newly free section, the three of us plop down in relief, continuing our conversation about the mysterious flowers I received this morning, though I didn't share the contents of the note with them. I'm not sure why I withheld that detail. Maybe concern that they'd spin it into meaning something more?

Something nefarious when my brain is already threatening to spiral down that road?

"Do yellow daisies hold some significance for you?" Caroline asks, sipping her iced mocha.

I shrug then reach into my crossbody purse for my keys, displaying one of the decorative pieces hanging from the metal ring. "Not particularly. I mean I've got this keychain from a trip my family took to the Daisy Festival years ago, but why would my parents randomly send me flowers? And for a festival that was just one of many family vacations?"

"Yeah, that doesn't make much sense." Amelie tilts her head to the side, contemplating the strange circumstances of my morning delivery. Her dance class wrapped early, so she was able to join us for a quick catch-up—not that our last chat was very long ago. Amelie is at the Reaper's Wolves compound almost as much as Caroline and I since she started dating Grim, one of the MC members.

"Let's not forget the obvious answer—Lindy's not-so-secret admirer."

"Ah, Timber... Are you two still playing like you aren't more than friends?" Amelie sits back in her chair with a huff of disbelief. The odd connection between the quiet giant MC member and I is a favorite subject for my book club friends. Not so much for me.

"We're not *playing* anything. We're just friends," I reiterate for the hundredth time.

"Friends don't act as your personal bodyguard, Lind. Always stepping in at the least hint of trouble."

"She's got a point," Caroline says. "He could be your *heart spark*. Your soulmate." The town legend is a favorite of hers since she fell in love with Snow, *her heart spark*. "Would it be so bad giving him a chance?"

Yes.

No.

I don't know.

"Can we talk about something else?" I beg, tired of thinking about the mysterious flowers and my potential feelings for Timber. Or vice versa. The man doesn't say much, so it's hard to tell where his head is at. He just appears when I need him.

'Might need him' is a fairer description of the times he's stepped between me and potential danger.

All Amelie and Caroline have to go off of are his actions, which admittedly may be stronger proof of his interest than mere words anyway. But I'm not dissecting theories about Timber's romantic interest, especially with so little to go on.

Caroline sighs but nods in agreement. "What are you going to do about Martha's message? Do you think you'll see her Friday night?"

Martha Chesson works for the same company Caroline and I do. We used to be acquaintances heading towards friends back when I worked in the office rather than remotely, but that was before I started distancing myself from people because of Dean.

He didn't like my attention split between him and anyone else, which included friends and family.

I don't know why I approached Caroline to help me leave Dean rather than Martha back then. Maybe it's because Caro was unavoidable with her desk being near the company entrance, so we saw each other every day without fail.

But Martha was easy to ghost since I knew when she ate lunch in the break room, and I took a different route to the bathrooms—one that avoided her cubicle. The interoffice IMs were a bit more difficult to ignore, but eventually, she stopped trying to hang out.

Until recently.

She heard about my breakup, probably by overhearing our boss talk about it since he had to approve my decision to work remotely—a choice made to create a clean break from Everton and Dean—and reached out.

"Yeah, I think so. It'll be good to rekindle those friendships I let die under Dean's control," I say.

Martha had messaged Caroline asking if she had my new number, then after checking with me, Caroline connected us. We've texted a couple of times to catch up before Martha asked if I'd like to hang out this Friday. Since I didn't have any plans—I rarely do outside of book club—I figured what the hell?

It's been over a year since I left Dean.

It's long past time for me to ease back into the social scene outside of Suitor's Crossing and the Reaper's Wolves MC community.

Caroline reaches across the table to squeeze my forearm. "I'm proud of you for putting yourself out there again. Martha and I weren't super close, but she seemed nice enough. Go have fun, then tell us all about it."

GO HAVE FUN. TELL US all about it. Caroline's words ring through my head as my gaze absorbs the scene around me.

I can't believe *this* is where Martha wanted to go—Rust, Everton's premiere underground bar and club. The large industrial space looks like it belongs in a horror film with all the stained concrete and eroded metal. An abandoned warehouse chic vibe clings to the building. The perfect place for all kinds of degenerates.

Okay, maybe, everyone isn't a delinquent, but still... This is a far cry from what I imagined tonight would be. I wanted to dip my toes into society again, not cannonball into shark-infested waters.

Where's the classy bartop, leather booths, and warm wooden features meant for a cozy atmosphere? My black bodycon dress rides up my thighs, and I hurriedly tug it down, regretting the decision to assume we were going somewhere upscale.

You know what they say about people who assume...

"Are you sure it's a good idea to be here? Is it safe?" I whisper to Martha. Her head bobs to the music filtering through the air as she scans the crowd of people in front of us.

The moment we parked outside Rust, I tried persuading her to go to Diamond instead. At least that club is owned by the Reaper's Wolves MC, making it leagues better in my mind.

But Martha was adamant that I give Rust a chance.

"Of course, just relax! Your ex must have done a real number on you if you're this antsy about a club. You really need to loosen up." Her hand pushes me forward once she finds who she's looking for.

I stumble a bit in my heels, unused to their added height, then recover, narrowing my eyes. She didn't shove hard, but I don't like even the pretense of being forced into something.

It's too reminiscent of Dean.

Martha introduces me to a group of six people occupying a dimly lit corner couch. Everyone scoots to the side so there's enough room for Martha to settle on the lumpy cushions, but it's clear I won't fit in the tiny space leftover. Not with my wide as fuck hips.

"I'll stand. Thanks." I wave off Martha's silently raised brow.

My plan is to recede into the background while she talks with her friends. I'll wait the night out in my own little corner until we leave, privately acknowledging that this will be the last time I ever hang out here. It might be the last time I meet up with Martha, too, if this is her idea of fun.

Sketchy warehouse clubs really don't fit her work vibe, but I guess that makes sense. People wear different facades depending on their environment. I just wish I'd seen beneath hers before agreeing to step into this bad idea waiting to happen.

CHAPTER FOUR

LINDY

I *don't feel too good.*

My head is pounding, and my stomach is threatening to revolt at any moment. Looking around Rust, I can't find Martha.

Where did she go?

Things were going smoothly in our little corner group. An actual waitress distributed bottles of ice cold beer, then there was more chatter before everything became fuzzy. Holding my half-empty bottle higher, I squint at the sloshing liquid.

Surely, this didn't get me drunk. It's less than we drink during one of our book club girls' nights.

Someone bumps my elbow in passing, and I careen forward before bracing against the wall. *Okay, breathe, maybe you need some fresh air to shake off the effects of the alcohol.* Focusing on my new destination, I slowly make my way to the door Martha and I entered hours ago.

Every few minutes I stop and rest, fearing I may really vomit in front of all these strangers, then start moving again once the nauseous feeling recedes.

Sweat gathers uncomfortably on my body. The ruched fabric of my dress itches, and I keep swallowing that distinctive flavor that coats your tongue before throwing up.

Just keep moving. Breathe.

Oh god, I need to sit down again.

Lurching toward an empty place on the wall, I accidently fall into a couple making out in the shadows.

Sorry, I think. My tongue feels too thick, making speech a struggle.

"Are you okay?" A girl asks from my periphery.

"I... I'm f—" Before I can finish my sentence, I collapse over one of the many barrels set up throughout the space. Whether they're purely decorative or actual trashcans doesn't matter to me as I hack up everything I've had tonight—the beer and a quick TV dinner of turkey and potatoes. A chill washes over me as I cling to the scratchy metal.

This is my home now.

Trapped and sick and so fucking alone.

Where the hell is Martha?

I should call Caroline.

Or Timber...

A shadow crosses over my white-knuckled hands.

It's the last thing I see before I finally pass out.

CHAPTER FIVE

TIMBER

D*amn. Shit. Fuck.* I catch Lindy before she hits the ground.

"Oh my god! What's wrong with her?" The woman clinging to her girlfriend studies Lindy's lax body with morbid curiosity.

Hefting Lindy higher against my chest, I ignore the question and head outside as Ranger and Grim trail my steps. It's pure coincidence that we're at Rust tonight. Despite the crowd, the club isn't doing too well, and the owner is looking to sell. With the recent loss of Club Wolf, the Reaper's Wolves have been debating rebuilding from scratch, but remodeling a standing structure like Rust might be better for us.

We'd just wrapped up our meeting with the owner when I spotted Lindy's familiar red head staggering across the club floor. It was obvious something was wrong from the unsteady way she walked, but I never expected her to collapse into a dead faint.

"Is she drunk? That doesn't seem like her," Ranger says from my side.

"No, it doesn't," I grit through clenched teeth. I caught the tailend of a conversation between Caroline and Snow at the clubhouse, where she mentioned Lindy hanging out with an old coworker tonight. The news had filled my gut with pride.

Lindy's stretching her wings past the safety of the MC and her book club friends. She's collecting the pieces of her past, rebuilding relationships—something that gives me hope for the future.

But I hate that her night out is ending like this. Passed out after puking her guts out.

The Reaper's Revamp truck is a welcome sight a few minutes later, as is the soft breeze blowing away the stench of sweaty bodies. I delivered a completed paint job before the Rust meeting, necessitating the larger vehicle versus my Harley, and I send up a prayer of thanks.

No way Lindy would've been able to ride home on the back of my bike with the way she's feeling.

She fidgets in my arms, slowly returning to consciousness.

"Easy, baby. I'm going to get you home, okay?"

"Timber?" she mumbles, her nose burrowing into my neck.

"I'm here."

Ranger swings the truck door open, and I gently place her on the faded seat. She huddles against the console, shivers wracking her body, so I grab a heavy jacket from the back. It's dirty and smells like gasoline, but it'll do for now. "Here, put this on. It might help warm you up."

"T... thanks." The misery in her tone wrenches at my heart. Carefully closing the door, I turn toward Ranger and Grim who've been watching silently.

"I'll make sure she gets home safely. You guys can leave. Let Snow know what we learned tonight. Rust sounds like a good investment," I say, trying to rein in my need to run to the driver's side and take off rather than discussing MC business like my attention isn't entirely on the sick woman behind me.

Ranger nods. "Don't worry about it. Take care of your girl." He and Grim dip their heads in farewell before straddling their bikes, and I round the hood of the truck to climb into the driver's seat.

Tears flow down Lindy's face, but the body-shaking chills seem to have slowed.

Fuck the forty-five-minute drive to Suitor's Crossing. Lindy doesn't need to suffer that long when the MC has an apartment ten minutes away. It's sparse—meant as a quick place to crash between Everton and Suitor's Crossing—but it'll do in a pinch.

After we're parked in front of the quiet building, Lindy wastes no time fumbling with her seatbelt, tossing the door open, and practically falling out of the cab. Loud retching reaches my ears as I stand like an idiot, unsure of what to do, until she finishes, trying to right herself but swaying forward instead. Wrapping her in my arms again, it's a short trek to the one-bedroom apartment situated on the first floor.

"Is this a stomach bug, Lind?"

It has to be, right? Lindy is too self-contained to get publicly drunk with someone she's only recently reconnected with. Even at club parties, her drinking doesn't exceed a beer or two.

"I don't know."

The bright bathroom lights cause us both to wince. Lindy sinks onto the closed toilet lid with a groan, and I wet a rag to wipe away the streaks of tears down her cheeks. My touch is gentle, but a part of me expects her to flinch at the intimacy.

I'm a scary motherfucker with rough hands and a rougher past who doesn't deserve to touch her. Especially when she's dealt with an abusive bastard like her ex.

That's one of the reasons I've held back for so long.

Even though I crave Lindy, I'm not sure it's what's best for her.

When I'm finished cleaning her up, I offer a new toothbrush and a cupful of mouthwash to rid her of the vomit aftertaste.

Little moans of pain periodically escape her throat. Small sounds that tear at something inside that I'd thought had died long ago.

I need her to stop. I can't take her cries of distress.

"Shhh... Lindy Girl, I've got you. You'll feel better soon. You're being so brave." I softly speak whatever comes to mind to distract her as my palm rubs soothing circles on her back.

This gentleness has been hiding my whole life, only manifesting upon meeting Lindy.

Maybe that's part of the Suitor's Crossing *heart sparks* legend. When you meet your soulmate, you inherently change, become better for them.

And Lindy deserves the best.

Despite her experience with that asshole Dean, she's an innocent—not jaded or cynical. Probably grew up in a healthy, loving home where she was given whatever she wanted because no one wanted to deny such a sweet girl.

It's a life I can't imagine.

As far back as I can remember, it's always been just me. My junkie mom dumped me at her alcoholic brother's at a young age, and my life never improved. Until I was old enough to defend myself against beatings from my uncle. Until I gathered enough money to move out at sixteen. Then enough determination to join the army at eighteen.

I grab a change of clothes from the closet full of random items left behind by past guests.

"Do you want me to call Caroline or Faith?" Maybe she'll feel more comfortable with a female presence rather than mine, considering how vulnerable she is in her current state.

Lindy gives me a blank look—off in her own head—probably trying to wrap her mind around tonight's events.

"No, I just want to sleep. I'll take the futon," she says wearily.

"You're taking the bed," I correct, guiding her toward the simple bedspread after she's changed and placing an empty trash bin beside the mattress in case she gets sick during the night.

I wouldn't call myself a gentleman, but I won't let Lindy sleep on the cramped futon. The bed isn't much more comfortable, but at least it has a pillow and a blanket.

"Thanks." Lindy gingerly lowers herself onto the bed. The club didn't spring for a bedframe and headboard, so it sits on the floor, and for the first time, I'm embarrassed by the bachelor pad. I wish I had something better to offer.

Once she's settled, my weary body contorts into an awkward shape on the futon to get some sleep, but my mind keeps circling around the woman who has hijacked my every waking thought for months.

A PIERCING CRY WAKES me from my light rest. Lindy tosses and turns beneath the thin blanket, every now and then letting out a fearful wail. Rolling to my feet, I hurry to the bed.

"It's just a dream. Wake up." My hand gently shakes her shoulder, trying to bring her back to reality. Instead, she twists to fight me, one of her fists glancing off my shoulder. It hardly makes an impact on my broad frame, but I quickly cover Lindy's body with mine to prevent her from accidently hurting herself.

I read once how pressure on the body releases some relaxing hormone. I'm not sure if it's true, but it's worth a shot. So, though Lindy attempts to buck my weight, I don't let up.

This could be doing more harm than good.

If she's having a nightmare, it could be about Dean, and having a giant man like me bearing down on her in her sleep could scare the shit out of her.

But what else can I do when she's flailing around the mattress locked in fear? Her fists knock against the wall behind her head before I capture them and hold them to the mattress.

I'll wait for Lindy to calm down, realize no one is here to harm her, then I'll let go. That's my haphazard plan. So while she's stuck in the throes of a nightmare, I go back to reassuring her.

"You're safe. No one's going to hurt you. I'm with you."

The three sentences become a litany, a promise, as she eventually relaxes under my weight. I'm not sure if it's the words or sheer exhaustion on her part, but I'll take it.

Anything is better than hearing the little whimpers emanating from her throat or watching her fight an invisible attacker.

I slowly inch my way off her, but as soon as she's free, Lindy begins fighting the air and crying out again.

A heavy sigh blows past my lips.

This is going to be a long night.

Returning to my protective post covering Lindy's body, my head rests next to hers as I repeat the cycle of whispering that she's safe—praying she'll resume a peaceful sleep while visions of the hundred different ways I could end Dean flash in my mind.

CHAPTER SIX

LINDY

U*nbearable heat.*
The scent of fresh pine.
What happened last night?

Timber's heavy body rests on top of me. I'm covered head to toe by him. His head between my breasts. One tattooed arm curled up my side to wrap underneath my shoulder. A long, muscular leg trapping mine against the bed.

This man has me completely at his mercy.

A panic attack should be gearing up at his close proximity—especially when I haven't had a man in my bed since Dean—but Timber has never turned his strength on me.

All that brute power? He's used it to save me from potentially dangerous situations time and again, instead.

He's been the perfect gentleman. Except for being in this bed right now.

How did we end up snuggled together?

My brain is still fuzzy although my stomach doesn't feel like it's going to revolt again. For a minute, I search for details of the previous night, but nothing comes to mind, and frankly, I'm still tired. It's too early to try to piece together what happened at Rust after Martha disappeared.

Letting it go for now, my eyes flutter shut as I shift into a more comfortable position. My range of motion is limited with Timber anchoring me to the mattress, but strangely, I don't mind.

A part of me likes where he is.

I feel comfortable and safe, even if it's a little hard to breathe and his body is like a fucking furnace. It's a small price to pay for the feeling of security.

I inwardly laugh at myself. A burly military veteran who also rides with a motorcycle club should scare the hell out of me, yet he represents safety.

Maybe my head's broken after the stress and abuse my ex put me through. Or my sense of who's safe in the world is warped since Dean was a fucking cop.

Timber huffs like he knows my thoughts are wandering into bad territory, and I let it distract me. The man sleeps like the dead, despite my moving around. He hasn't readjusted the whole time I've been awake.

Must be nice being able to sleep that deeply.

I usually wake up a few times a night from tossing and turning and more recently bad dreams. They've improved with therapy and distance from Dean, but they still lurk in the depths of my mind, primed to emerge when I least expect it.

Maybe Timber's presence can protect me from those, too...

CHAPTER SEVEN

TIMBER

I fell asleep during my watch over Lindy. Like a fucking amateur. Like I hadn't stayed awake for days at a time in the military.

Unplanned as it was, though, it resulted in one of the best nights I've had in awhile. Lindy's body is heaven compared to a mattress. Her softness and warmth wrapped around me and calmed my restless thoughts in record time.

Especially since my sleep schedule usually consists of a few hours each night, because I can never let go enough to be completely vulnerable even in my sleep. At least once a week, I pass out from sheer exhaustion and sleep-deprivation. *Those* are normally my best nights.

But even that doesn't compare to sleeping with Lindy.

Somehow, in the process of comforting her, she returned the favor without even trying. I slept like a fucking baby and woke nestled between her breasts to prove it.

When I realize where I am, why I actually had been dreaming, I'm stunned. This woman managed to do the impossible in her sleep.

So, naturally, rather than exiting the bed like a gentleman, I stay like a fucking creeper and study her relaxed features, trying to figure out what her magic is.

Wild curls spread out on the pillow like blooming vines of scarlet. I reach out to touch one, and it immediately captures my finger, then after a gentle tug, it springs back into shape upon release.

Faint freckles lay scattered across her cheeks, painting a direct trail to her pretty mouth, slightly parted with each slow breath.

My morning wood continues to harden the longer I look at those perfectly heart-shaped lips, so I glance away, soaking in the rest of her body that's hidden under the borrowed clothes.

Dammit.

That's not doing anything to calm my blood either. Because while she may be blocked from my eyes, I still feel every curve under my body. Remember being cushioned by her full breasts.

Like she hears my inner struggle, Lindy shifts, which cocoons my cock between her lush thighs. A strangled groan escapes my throat as it takes all my strength not to push a little deeper.

Get up and move, pussy.

Fuck, don't think about pussy...

Because now my mind is filled with an image of what Lindy's would look like. Pretty, pink... wet for my tongue. *Fuck.* I jump out of bed, grab my discarded jeans, and run to the kitchen to put distance between us.

CHAPTER EIGHT

LINDY

I'm not sure how much time passes before my eyes open again, but the heavy weight of Timber is gone, bringing a surprising amount of regret with the realization.

"I'd take it easy if I were you. You had a rough night." A low voice calls from the kitchen as I sit up. Timber fills a glass with water before finding a bottle of pills in one of the drawers.

"Take these." He quickly drops the items on the floor by my head then shuffles away.

"Thanks. Where am I?" I wince at the rough sound of my voice. *I never want to throw up again.*

"In an apartment the club owns. We keep it on hand for when someone needs to be in Everton for a prolonged amount of time, or if they're too tired to make the drive back to Suitor's Crossing. Snow decided it was a good idea after Caroline's accident."

He leans against the kitchen counter and crosses his arms, causing his tattoos to ripple over the firm muscles. An expression of concern furrows his brows. "Do you remember anything about last night?"

"Only feeling awful. Did I pass out?"

Nodding his head, he gestures toward my phone on the carpet.

Why is this bed missing a frame?

"Your phone's been blowing up with messages since I let Snow and Caroline know what happened." There's a pause. "No judgment, but how much did you drink?"

"Half a beer, so not enough to warrant my body's reaction. Is it possible to get a bad batch?" I ask, remembering the local label on the bottle. My knowledge of breweries is basically zero, but I can't think of any other explanation for feeling sick. Stomach bugs don't usually appear then vanish within such a limited timespan.

After downing the ibuprofen, I skim my most recent texts and type out quick replies. Caroline and the rest of the girls can get the full story in-person when I'm not so groggy.

"I'm not sure. Maybe you were sensitive to one of the ingredients. But you're feeling better now?"

"Yeah, and the medicine should get rid of the remnants of a headache..." I trail off as I study the small apartment. There isn't much to it. Besides the kitchen table and chairs, the mattress lies on the floor, while a futon and a TV sitting on an overturned milk crate reside in the living room.

This really is just a pitstop for the MC guys.

Timber clears his throat. "I'm going to shower real quick, then we can hit the road. If you need anything, it'll be here." His hand waves around the kitchen then he leaves.

Not much of a talker.

But I knew that already.

"I'm going to lay back down. See if anything comes to mind about last night."

Crawling back under the blanket, I consciously avoid watching Timber head to the bathroom for a shower. He's going to be naked just on the other side of that thin door, and not for the first time, I wonder how far his tattoos extend.

Forget it. Now's not the time to salivate over Timber.

You're not looking for a relationship anytime soon, remember?

There's no harm in looking.

As my brain wages an internal war with my hormones, I punch the lumpy pillow and try to get comfortable. I must have really been out of it last night because, normally, I could never sleep with one measly pillow and a not-thick-at-all cover.

I like to be buried beneath as many pillows and heavy blankets as possible.

Guess Timber was a worthy substitute.

CHAPTER NINE

TIMBER

When Lindy woke up, I kept the kitchen table between us to disguise the obvious bulge tenting my sweatpants. I don't think she noticed it during my short sprint between the kitchen and the bed to drop off the water and meds or during our conversation, which should have been enough to rein it in.

But the motherfucker refused to deflate while in the same room as Lindy.

So, a shower seemed like a good idea. Something to cool me down.

I toss my clothes onto the white tile, hop into the slim stall, and turn the water to the coldest setting.

And the biting chill doesn't do a damn thing to douse my arousal.

Damn. Shit. Fuck.

Desperate for a reprieve, no matter how much of a pervert it makes me, I soap up my body and grab my cock. It started leaking pre-cum the moment I thought of Lindy's pussy, so my dick's already a fucking slippery mess without the soapy lubricant.

Bracing one hand on the beige wall, I imagine Lindy on her knees in front of me. Waiting to drink down everything I give her.

I stroke harder at the thought of her mouth sucking my dick. Licking it like she loves every inch of it, and my own mouth salivates thinking about her cream coating my tongue. I'd eat her out, then like a good girl, she'd return the favor—but not out of obligation, out of sheer need.

My breathing stutters as I give one more firm squeeze at that visual, and I come hard. Ropes of cum splatter the shower floor and wall as I lean against it to catch my breath. *Holy hell.* That was a damn sexy fantasy.

If only I can make it real some day...

Adjusting the temperature so warm water runs down my body, I wash away the evidence of my jerking off.

Then berate myself.

What the fuck am I thinking? Hell will freeze over before Lindy lets me put my hands on her curves—or my dick in her sweet mouth... or tight pussy.

Goddammit.

My cock rallies for a second round but I ignore it. I focus on roughly scrubbing myself down and getting the hell out of the shower before there's a repeat performance.

Stop thinking about fucking Lindy.

She's had a tough night—a tough year, to be honest.

But so have I when it comes to my girl. I've struggled to get her out of my head for months.

How can I ignore her now when she's just on the other side of the door?

Warm in the bed we shared?

Easy. Remember how much you don't want to scare her off and keep your dick in your pants.

CHAPTER TEN

LINDY

Giving up on jogging my memory of last evening, I get up and head to the kitchen to see what's available for breakfast. It's the least I can do to thank Timber for keeping me safe in the crowd of strangers at Rust.

A white light highlights the empty refrigerator shelves aside from basic milk, eggs, butter, and a six pack of beer. The cabinets don't offer much more except for bread and some other staple items.

"Okay... A simple breakfast it is," I drawl, collecting the ingredients for scrambled eggs and toast. There's one lone pan in a lower cabinet, so I start heating that up on the stove as I grab two plates. They're mismatched plastic circles—most likely the dollar ones from WalMart.

The Reaper's Wolves really didn't spend much to make this a comfortable place to stay. Every guest is forced to live off the bare necessities.

Humming that song in my head, I push the sleeves of my borrowed hoodie to my elbows and whisk the eggs and milk with a fork before pouring the prepared mixture into the pan.

After they're all fluffed and seasoned with salt and pepper I discovered in a drawer, I split the eggs on the two plates, giving Timber the majority. When I turn to toast the bread—my mind focused on remembering the next lyrics to the old childhood song—the man in question is standing in the bathroom doorway, eyeing me curiously.

I have a slight McSteamy moment with his low-riding black sweatpants and semi-transparent white tee. Tattoos decorate most of his bulky frame, tapering down his muscular chest, and it's a sight to behold. So much so, my gaze refuses to tear itself away from the temptation of deciphering the images beneath the flimsy cotton.

Quit ogling him!

"I'm making breakfast," I squeak before clearing my throat, whipping back toward the toaster. "Consider it a thank you."

Timber doesn't respond, just sits down at the dining table with a confused look on his face. He seems more wary than he was before the shower.

"For keeping me safe last night," I clarify.

Our toast pops up, and I breathe a sigh of relief that it isn't too dark. I adjusted the toaster settings, but one can never be too certain. A memory of Dean tossing out my effort to make him a birthday breakfast flashes in my mind, but I shove it away.

Adding a few pieces to Timber's plate, I place it in front of him along with the butter and a knife.

"Do you want water or milk to drink?" I ask as I search for cups. They aren't hard to find since there's hardly anything *to* find.

His chair scrapes across the vinyl flooring as he prepares to fill his own glass when I stop him with a hand on his arm. "I'll get it. This is your thank you, remember?"

He pauses then mumbles, "Milk."

After setting his drink in front of him, I do a quick kitchen clean-up then join him at the small table with my breakfast.

It doesn't look like he's touched anything yet.

Freaking out a little, I shove a bite of eggs into my mouth to make sure they're edible, but they taste fine to me.

That doesn't mean anything.

Dean could always find problems.

Damn, yesterday really messed with my head if Dean's invading my thoughts so thoroughly.

With the help of therapy and the support of my friends, my mental health has improved drastically since leaving my ex, and I don't think of him nearly as often as I used to. But between seeing him at the Club Wolf fire, receiving those mystery flowers, and puking my guts out yesterday, the ghost of Dean has weaseled its way back into my head.

"Are you okay? Is something wrong?" I ask. This whole situation feels awkward. Somehow our roles have reversed. Now, *I'm* making sure *he's* alright when I don't understand what could've gone wrong.

My questions shake him from wherever he was because he begins eating, and I follow suit. Things are quiet—even our forks against the plates don't make much sound.

Usually, I prefer a peaceful calm, but this is a little unnerving.

I don't like feeling like I'm walking on eggshells around a person. I've done enough of that to last a lifetime.

"It must be handy having this place in town, huh?" Not the most interesting question, but it's all I can think of. Generally, I'm not the one having to pull information out of people.

They're all too happy to provide it themselves with no prompting, except for Timber.

He nods but doesn't elaborate.

Okay...

CHAPTER ELEVEN

TIMBER

When I finished my shower and stepped out to see Lindy standing in the kitchen making breakfast, shock coursed through me. I wasn't sure what to make of the scene, especially since shame battered my insides after jerking off to thoughts of her.

In my experience, whenever someone does something nice for me, they always expect repayment, but Lindy doesn't need anything from me.

Except your cock.

After slamming the door on that unhelpful thought, I'd watched as she mixed something in a bowl, giving a frustrated sigh every time she had to stop to push up the too-big sleeves of her hoodie. An unfamiliar feeling had unfurled inside me—a healing warmth.

In my messed up life, no one has ever made me breakfast. And how pathetic is that? Sure, the biker bunnies who hang out at the clubhouse will sometimes make a huge communal breakfast, but it's not specifically for me.

Not like this.

My drunken uncle relied on a steady diet of alcohol, so I was always left to my own devices. I grew up malnourished and skinny, until I learned the art of stealing. As soon as I figured out how to grab a loaf of bread here or a bottle of orange juice there, the constant hunger had been kept at bay.

It's a miracle I made it to eighteen without a criminal record and was able to join the army, which quickly straightened me out. Of course, it helped that I had three regular meals a day.

Breakfast is a quiet affair due to the swirl of emotions knotting my gut. It's like I've forgotten how to act around Lindy. Or at least how to talk to her.

Not that we've spent a ton of time engaging in small talk when I'm not much for long conversations in the first place.

But actions speak louder than words, right?

And it's always been easier for me to act.

"I'll wash the dishes." Gathering our empty plates and cups, I stride toward the kitchen sink, grateful for a task to occupy my hands—one that doesn't involve testing the silkiness of Lindy's skin.

"I can help. It's not like there's much to do," she chirps.

"Which means I can handle it myself. You cooked, so I'll clean. If you haven't already, why don't you let your friends know that we'll be back in Suitor's Crossing soon?"

Her eyes narrow at my abrupt tone, and I instantly want to apologize for my gruffness. I'm not upset with her. I'm frustrated with myself.

"Alright..." She slowly nods, staying at the dining table while I scrub our plates.

Fifteen minutes later, I lock up the apartment, and we start the journey home. Lindy rolls her window down, negating the ability to chat, which I'm thankful for. Besides, autumn is upon us, and the crisp chill is a welcome balm to my frayed nerves.

Frayed nerves, I inwardly scoff. *I sound like a Victorian spinster calling for her smelling salts.* That's the last time I stay to watch a movie with the guys and their women.

Once we're at Lindy's cabin, I walk her to the front door, gravel crunching beneath our feet.

A bright spot of yellow catches my eye. Flower petals. A few are trapped between the welcome mat and porch. The florist refused to share anything about the person who sent the bouquet when I visited, so I still have no clue who else is interested in my girl.

But the reminder of Lindy's secret admirer prompts me to do the dumbest thing of my life.

"Would you have dinner with me?" I ask, shoving a hand in my back pocket.

Her terrified face is answer enough.

Of course.

No way would she go out with me. Not after the horrible evening she had. Not after her abusive ex.

Lindy probably won't be ready to date for a long time yet.

I don't know what the hell I was thinking—letting a few flower petals make me jealous—because my timing fucking sucks.

"You're right. Nevermind, sorry I asked," I mutter, turning away.

Stupid, fucking idiot, delusional...

"Wait!" Lindy grabs my arm. "Dinner would be nice." Her shy smile causes a tiny ray of hope to bloom inside me.

"Would it? Because I saw your face when I asked. It's hard to mask that kind of reaction. Don't say yes out of obligation. It's okay to say no."

I never want to force Lindy into anything.

Heat flushes her cheeks. "Sorry about that. It just came out of nowhere. I wasn't expecting you to ask me out, and when you did, I didn't know how to react. That's what you saw on my face." Her eyes close as she tilts her head upward then looks back at me with embarrassment. "I'm not used to it."

"Used to what?"

Lindy's discomfort increases as she looks anywhere but me. "Being asked out. Going on dates."

Bewilderment fills my mind. How is that even possible? She's a perfect match for some boy next door. She's sexy and smart, kind and adorable. Who could resist that?

I stare at Lindy, lost for words.

"I know. I'm weird. You're the first man to ask me out since Dean, but even before him, I never really dated much."

"You're not weird. Everyone else is apparently blind and stupid. Does tomorrow night work for you?" That might be too soon, but I don't want to waste any more time. She's giving me a chance, and I'm not going to blow it.

"Perfect," she agrees, smiling in relief.

"I'll pick you up at six tomorrow."

Then I leave with a fucking bounce in my step. *Happy*. I can't remember the last time I truly felt that way.

CHAPTER TWELVE

LINDY

I pace the cabin porch waiting for Timber to pick me up for our date. All day, I've been mentally patting myself on the back for agreeing to go out with him, especially after my disastrous attempt to reenter the social world this past weekend.

Unsure how casual this dinner date would be, I erred on the side of caution and dressed up in an autumn-patterned sundress that flows around me every time I walk.

The dress has a silk under layer since the overlay is sheer chiffon, and the buttoned bodice creates the perfect amount of modest cleavage. *Well, sort of modest.* I've gained weight since first buying the dress, and it shows in the way my chest overflows the top. But at least the fluttery skirt glides over the rest of my added roundness.

A cloud of dust follows Timber's car down the gravel drive. He parks in front of the cabin and gets out before I can hop in the passenger seat.

It's unexpected since I'm already outside, negating the need for knocking on my door, but he moves to stand in front of me, and after a brief, "Damn," as he surveys my outfit, he offers a bouquet of flowers.

"I wasn't sure what you'd like, but I figured I should bring something, so um, here you go."

That's unexpectedly sweet of him.

Biting my lower lip, I accept the gift, appreciating its difference from the mysterious delivery I received a few days ago. This one is filled with tulips rather than daisies and some other flowers I can't name.

"Well, you guessed correctly because I love tulips. Most people may prefer roses or whatever, but I've always liked these." I gently rub a velvety petal between my fingers. I've always had an affinity for these simple but pretty flowers. "Hang on while I put these in water."

I rush inside, leaving Timber to stand awkwardly on the porch. I don't have a vase, so I fill a large cup with water instead. Later I'll buy a vase and cut the stems, but right now I have a sweet man waiting for me.

Sweet.

Who'd have thought I'd ever describe one of the Reaper's Wolves men that way?

Who'd have thought I'd accept a date when just days ago I was trying to convince myself that I'm not interested in a romantic relationship?

Once I return, Timber gestures ahead of him, matching my steps to the passenger side to open the door for me.

This gentlemanly part of him is a pleasant surprise.

Is this how Snow, Alaska, and Grim treat their women, my friends?

No wonder they fell so hard.

Being treated with kindness and respect shouldn't be so earth-shattering—it's the bare minimum on how to treat a person—but a wave of unexpected tears catch me off guard, until I blink them away.

No one's put this much effort in for me in a long time.

Once Timber buckles in beside me, he drives us to an Italian restaurant on Main Street, where we're immediately seated at a table for two by the window. The waiter hands us menus then leaves after listing the specials.

The prices are no joke. I could buy meals for a whole day with what an entrée costs here.

And just like that, I become self-conscious about what to order. Timber must've known about the cost of the place before bringing me here, but what if he didn't? What if he had seen this place randomly and thought he'd try it out?

That happened once to Dean and I. We'd gone out to a fancy new restaurant to show off for his buddies. He loved having the finer things in life even if it was out of reach financially. It had been nerve-wracking witnessing his temper rise as I cautiously ordered, attempting and failing to land on the correctly priced items for him to remain calm.

In the end, I'd ended up paying for part of the entire meal along with a tip because his pride wouldn't hear of his buddies shelling out the cash. That would defeat the purpose of bragging about his ability to host a get-together at the classy restaurant.

Timber's not Dean, but I don't want him humiliated by a large bill he can't afford.

"Is everything okay? If you don't like Italian, we can go somewhere else."

"What...?" My eyes guiltily flick upward as if he knew exactly where my thoughts were. "No, Italian's good."

"So, what are you thinking? Because you're frowning." His observation jolts me into full recovery mode.

I paste a bright smile on my face. "Just debating my choices. Call it RDF: resting decision face." It's not my best work, but it seems to appease him as I mention how good the cheapest item on the menu looks—a salad with baked chicken on top.

I'll be hungry afterwards, but at least it'll be for a good cause.

Timber reads the meal description aloud. "Are you sure? You can get whatever you want. It's fine."

"That is what I want. Is there something wrong with a salad?"

He shakes his head, and my shoulders drop in relief.

The waiter returns for our order, saving me from the awkward moment. I go first then Timber follows by ordering a steak and asking if I want any wine. After I decline, the waiter leaves to place our orders.

We sit in silence as I try tallying what the cost of our meal will be.

Timber's not destitute, but I don't think he's loaded with cash either.

"You look beautiful, you know. I think I was supposed to say that when I first saw you, but I was too awestruck." The hesitant tone of his low voice draws my attention. It almost sounds like he's shy.

Is that possible?

Tingles erupt at the compliment. No one has ever called me beautiful. I'm cute, pretty on occasion, but never beautiful. And Dean never believed in compliments—unless they were the backhanded kind—once the 'honeymoon' period of our relationship wore off.

I smile in gratitude and study Timber. Slacks with a navy button down shirt. No tie, so the open collar displays the tattoos climbing his strong neck. His beard even looks freshly trimmed.

"You clean up well yourself," I praise, ducking my head even as I lean towards him.

A handsome grin brightens his harsh features, and the ice is finally broken as we settle into a normal conversation. One that isn't stilted and cautious like most of our interactions this weekend.

When our food arrives, the portion sizes are huge, dismissing another worry of mine. *Looks like I won't go home hungry, after all.*

After we finish and decline the dessert offering, the waiter brings the check, and I restrain myself from sneaking a peek at the total, though I offer to split the meal cost.

He gives me a firm, "Hell no."

Then proves I had nothing to be concerned about because he pulls out his card and places it in the little check holder without a second glance.

I should've known everything would be alright, but hard-taught lessons are difficult to overcome.

Time to work through another Dean-centered issue in my therapy sessions.

Yippee...

"Do you want to go home? Or are you open to heading somewhere else first?" Timber asks once we're settled in his vehicle.

I opt for the second choice since it's still early in the evening, and things are actually going well between us. As he drives, I return to our previous topic. "You were in Everton for a Reaper's Revamp delivery?"

"Yep, the customer needed it for a car show this afternoon but a last minute errand took longer than expected, so he couldn't pick it up himself."

"How did you get involved with classic car restorations? Weren't you in the military like the rest of the MC guys?"

He thinks about his answer before replying, an edge to his voice. "My uncle kept a '69 Chevy Camaro locked in the garage. It didn't run and had a shit paint job from his amateur attempt to restore it. I always wanted to fix the car myself and use it to escape, but the bastard was damn particular about that vehicle. It's the one thing he cared about other than booze."

"So, I read a ton of car manuals," he flashes a wry grin my way, "Riveting stuff, I tell you, and memorized a lot of knowledge. During my service, I put some of that to use. We didn't have classic cars but some of those military-issued jeeps and trucks were old as fuck. Everything snowballed into Reaper's Revamp once I hooked up with the Reaper's Wolves MC."

"Wow, impressive, though I'm sorry about your uncle. He sounds like an asshole." Men like that are all too familiar. "I've never been handy with cars. I've probably been suckered into spending thousands more than necessary whenever a mechanic says I need something fixed."

"Not anymore," Timber growls. "If you run into car trouble or even if you just need an oil change, let me know. No one's going to take advantage of you again."

I resist the urge to fidget in my seat. His solemn promise has me feeling some sort of way because sincerity rings through every word.

Timber parks outside of an abandoned building at the edge of town. It doesn't look like much with its broken windows and boarded up entrances. In fact, it looks like a place where people are murdered and dumped.

Club Rust 2.0.

"Come on, don't be afraid. It'll be worth it, I promise." Timber holds his hand out for me, a hopefulness clinging to his expression. "I swear you'll be safe. You have nothing to worry about."

"If you say so..." A hesitant chuckle masks my sudden nerves.

It's not that I distrust Timber. He's done nothing to set off alarm bells in my head or heart. Nothing in the entire fourteen months I've known him.

But this building is still fucking creepy.

I place my cold hand into his warm, rough palm, and he gives it an encouraging squeeze before leading me inside. We climb concrete stairs, overstepping trash and fallen debris until we reach the top, and Timber lets go to peek out the door.

I'm not sure what he's checking for, but he must see it because he leans back in and tells me to close my eyes.

"Trust me."

I feel like Jasmine being led by Aladdin.

It worked out for her, didn't it?

Sighing, my lashes slowly slide shut.

Timber takes both of my hands and guides me until, by the sound of things, we're outside again. His body shifts behind me, and a frisson of fear snaps to attention before I squash it.

He's not going to hurt me.

Before my brain can launch a full-scale rebuttal to that belief, his whispered breath ghosts over the back of my head.

"Open your eyes."

They widen at the sight before me. The sun is setting over Suitor's Crossing, peeking through the mountains guarding its western side. The pink and orange colors wash everything in a soft, flattering light, and this building has the perfect vantage point for it all.

"How'd you know about this place?" I ask in awe. Clearly, the warehouse's dilapidated demeanor dissuades visitors—it practically shouts *Stay out!*—yet Timber ignored the warning and discovered a slice of beauty amid the garbage.

He shrugs. "I found it on one of my long cruises around town. It's easier to think up here." His boot rests against the edge of the building.

"Makes sense. It's pretty peaceful... Once you get past the dangerous downstairs," I joke as I bump his elbow with mine.

"Yeah, this probably wasn't a good idea for a first date, now that you mention it. But hell..." Timber runs a hand through his hair. "I have no idea what I'm doing when it comes to these things. Or you, for that matter."

I'm taken aback by his uncertainty. The whole night he's been calm, confident, except for those tiny snippets of hesitancy to show he was more than just a giant, unshakeable bodyguard. He's human, too, with all the vulnerable emotions I have. The only difference is Timber hides them ninety-percent of the time.

Maybe because he feels he has to around me?

I admit his stoic and strong presence has always made me feel safe, but this gentler side is endearing, too. It doesn't detract from the alpha protective vibe he's usually got going on. It adds to it.

"You've been doing fine so far, including this stop," I say, licking my lips. His brown eyes drop to the motion. "I can't tell at all that you're new to this. Besides, I'm new, too."

A half-smile tugs at the corner of his mouth. "Which means you wouldn't know a bad date from a good one."

"Trust me, Timber, I'd know. I haven't been living in a convent all my life." And Dean's dates revolved around him schmoozing at upscale bars or skiing resorts. Wherever he could go and have people fawn over his role as a 'civil servant'—my eyes threaten to roll heavenward at the reminder—or build connections with the people who could advance his career.

Timber's not like that at all, based on the way he keeps checking in to see how I feel.

This date is about *me*.

CHAPTER THIRTEEN

GIDEON

I take her word for it. As long as Lindy is having a good time, that's all that matters to me.

"Call me Gideon," I say, anxious to hear my real name on her tongue. Probably should have said something when I picked her up hours ago. Or mentioned it during one of the dozen times we were at the clubhouse together.

"Gideon. Like Criminal Minds."

"Until he left."

"That's one of the few times a replacement character didn't suck," she says.

"You've got me there. Rossi's a cool dude." I'm impressed I'm able to hold up part of this conversation considering the distraction of Lindy wetting her lips.

The pretty shine begs me to have a taste, but I resist temptation, giving Lindy another onceover, instead, as we resume our posts watching the sunset.

She's so goddamned gorgeous.

Her dress looks like it could blow away with a strong breeze, and her tits... *Damn.* They're spilling over the top, eager for attention. Which I would gladly give if she didn't have me so tied in knots wondering how far is *too* far.

But that doesn't stop me from staring. I've been hard all evening—in perpetual discomfort—just by being near her. It's like I'm a teenager who doesn't know how to control himself.

Do not ruin tonight by pouncing on her like a hungry wolf.

Night falls as the last of the sun's rays disappear. When Lindy shivers from the drop in temperature, I reluctantly suggest leaving, and we slowly make our way downstairs.

I keep one hand on Lindy the whole time, pretending to help her around the littered building. In truth, I just want a reason to touch her before our date ends.

Unfortunately, the return journey to the Reaper's Wolves compound and her cabin takes less time than I want. Even after driving a little under the speed limit to prolong our time together.

"Tonight was fun," Lindy says, unbuckling her seat belt once I've parked. "Thank you for dinner and for sharing your special place."

I nod as she gets out of the car. Frozen. What do I do now? Walk her to the door? Kiss her?

Would she even let me?

Scrubbing a hand down my face, I remain silent, not even a fucking good night. *What the hell is wrong with me?* I'm not this guy. Second-guessing myself. Not taking what I want.

Good or bad, I make a decision and call out to Lindy. She turns at the slam of my car door, and I don't stop moving toward her until she's in my arms.

"What—"

I crush my mouth to hers, swallowing the surprise as her hands land on my shoulders, and we stumble back on her porch until the front door stops our forward trajectory.

My tongue roughly abrades hers, sweeping in and out, mimicking the dance of our bodies beneath the yellow porch light. Lindy moans and scrambles for purchase. Her nails scraping along my neck. A leg wrapping around my hips to hold me tighter.

At the evidence of her acceptance, I groan in victory and slide one hand behind her plump thigh, pulling her hard against my arousal as the other tries unbuttoning her bodice. Except the tiny buttons are impossible for my large fingers.

Fuck it.

I jerk the thin fabric down to reveal an even flimsier bra. The burgundy lace does nothing to hide the hardened buds begging for attention. My teeth catch one lace-covered nipple then gently nibble, a growl of satisfaction erupting from my chest like a beast in the midst of claiming its mate.

"Gideon..."

My name sounds breathy on her lips. Breathy and perfect. I want Lindy to repeat it—over and over—as I pleasure her curvy little body. Lowering a bra cup, I suckle the sensitive flesh to soothe my bite, my cock grinding deeper into her pussy.

I want Lindy to come.

Here on the porch with my name ringing through the air.

"Gideon," she pants. "We shouldn't..."

I switch nipples and continue to lash the pebbled buds with my tongue, letting my teeth graze her. Each time, she jumps a little, then redoubles her efforts to get closer to me. I want Lindy completely out of her mind with need. A need I intend to satisfy.

"Come on, Lindy Girl," I whisper as I rub my shadow-roughened cheek against her silky skin. I'm practically fucking her with my cock. All that separates us are my jeans and her soaked panties beneath the raised skirt of her dress.

My hand delves between us to circle her clit under the drenched fabric. She's so fucking wet I'll probably have a dark spot on my jeans from her cream, but I don't care.

I only crave her pleasure.

"I want to hear you cry out my name when you come," I growl in her ear, tugging on the lobe with my teeth. "I want you to scream it so loud everyone knows who you belong to."

"Oh, f..." Her heavy breathing hitches as I thrust one last time between her thighs, then she gives me exactly what I want—my name tumbling from her lips as her orgasm takes over. The waves contract around my fingers as I dip inside her pussy, keeping an easy rhythm to draw out her pleasure for as long as possible.

"Fuck, Lindy." I kiss beneath her ear. Along her jawline. "You're so beautiful, baby. So damn pretty when you come for me."

She rests her head against the cabin as she comes back down. Her eyes are closed, her chest struggling to resume its regular rhythm. I slip my hand from between us and suck my fingers clean before setting her to rights.

Damn, she tastes good.

A tinge of regret passes at the missed opportunity of tasting her sweet juices right at the source. *Next time.* The thought floats through my mind as Lindy opens her eyes again.

A look of horror crosses her face before she frantically shoves me away.

"Oh, God," she moans in despair, and a sinking feeling settles in my gut. "What have I done? Oh my God. We just...

You... I..." Lindy motions around her as one hand rubs circles on her reddened chest, raw from my bearded face burying itself in her soft breasts. "No, no..."

My hand raises to cup her cheek, but she stops me.

Tears well below her lashes. "Don't! Don't touch me."

"Lindy..." Fear courses through me. I didn't mean to make her cry.

She dodges my outstretched hand again, and I finally take a step back to give her space.

This can't be happening.

Tell me I didn't fuck this up already.

"I'm sorry. I should've taken things slower. Next time..."

"There will not be a next time," she declares as the tears fall. "This shouldn't have happened."

"Baby, I promise we can take things slow. I wasn't thinking clearly tonight. It's my fault. Just give me another chance," I plead.

Please don't go.

Please don't shut me out.

"It's both of our faults. I just—I—I'm sorry." With that, she runs. She fumbles with her house key before falling inside and slamming the door behind her.

I spin around and slam my fist on the porch railing, relishing the pain. My head hangs low above the grainy wood as I try to regain control of the hurricane of emotions whipping through me.

I had one good thing.

One.

And I fucked it up because I couldn't keep my hands off Lindy. I overcorrected from too cautious to too aggressive.

Now, she'll never let me touch her again.

CHAPTER FOURTEEN

LINDY

Hypersexuality.

It can be a symptom of abuse. A way for someone to regain control of their body. I learned about it in therapy, although I hadn't experienced it until now.

When I clawed at Gideon for more, and he gave it back to me in spades.

Before I freaked the fuck out.

These stupid tears blur my vision as I grab my sleep clothes and rush to the bathroom—a jumble of emotions manifesting in a fucking sobfest. Probably scared the shit out of Gideon.

I hiccup in embarrassment. He didn't deserve the way I acted after the best orgasm of my life. But in the moment, it was all too much.

Undressing, I catch sight of myself in the mirror. Gideon left his mark on my body. Small bruises form on my thigh where he held me and dark red blotches are spread across my chest. My lips are puffy and slightly sore from his possessive kisses.

Tracing the love bite on my neck, my nipples tighten again at the memory of his hot mouth devouring me like I was worth more than his next breath.

Wetness seeps from between my thighs.

God, how am I still this aroused?

I just had my first not self-given orgasm in forever, yet my body is desperate for more.

But it's too soon, right?

Yes, Gideon can be kind, but I don't need a burly military veteran who is also part of a motorcycle club. Someone who could break my heart.

Didn't I remind myself that I'm not risking myself again for any man after that mysterious flower delivery?

And yet... I can't stop thinking about him.

"Even before tonight," I mutter to myself.

His protective nature, always a few steps away, ready to jump in at the first hint of danger to me. His silent demeanor, always watching and listening, rather than puffing his chest and talking over people.

And let's not forget the freakishly strong attraction I have for him. I've never felt this way around a man. I've always hovered around lukewarm and figured that was as good as it was going to get.

But Gideon's tattoos, beard, leather cut, motorcycle... Geez, I could list every single hot as hell thing about him for ages, and all of it would add up to being as far from lukewarm as possible.

I'm a fucking supernova when it comes to him.

For months, I've been drifting through the icy universe—lost in a blackhole—with Gideon orbiting around me until this week when we finally collided. Shattering my rocky shell to reveal the white hot light beneath.

Confused and excited, I jump into the shower and turn the water temperature to scalding, hoping it'll burn out the different kind of heat pervading my body.

The wash sponge scrubs my skin hard, trying to erase the effect Gideon had on me, to no avail. My body still trembles at the thought of his hands running over me.

Might as well give in. Who will know?

Closing my eyes, I brush my fingers over my breasts. Pinching the swollen nipples, I imagine his teeth biting down like earlier.

The small pain makes way for pleasure as my breathing picks up. Reaching one hand down, I draw my finger across my clit before drifting further to drag some of my wetness up, trying to recreate the same sensations Gideon brought out in me.

As my climax nears, I speed up, rubbing harder.

Soon, the familiar crest of an orgasm surfaces, and I lean against the shower wall.

That was... nice.

But much weaker than what Gideon gave me.

How is that possible?

Why do I need a man, specifically *this* man, to achieve such pleasure?

"Get it together, Lindy!" I berate myself. Feminists everywhere are probably screaming at me for these thoughts. *I* should be screaming at me, but all I want is Gideon.

Banging my head against the tile, I groan in annoyance and regret.

Because why would he still want me after I cried and ran away from him like a scared little rabbit?

CHAPTER FIFTEEN

GIDEON

The week after my fuck-up was spent working and drinking at the clubhouse parties, where Lindy remained conspicuously absent. It passed in a blur of no sleep and anger at myself.

I can't believe I'd been stupid enough to think taking Lindy up against the cabin would be okay. A fucking cabin. Where anybody from the club could see.

A decent man would've walked her to her door and left it at that. He wouldn't have forced himself on her like a fucking animal.

The punching bag in front of me swings with another blow from my fist. I thought coming to Alaska's gym might help relieve some of my self-disgust, but so far it isn't working.

Lindy's tear-stained face fills my mind as I punch harder. Christ, I made her cry. My rough fucking hands. My punishing teeth and kisses. They caused her enough pain to cry.

I probably reminded her of her asshole ex.

I hit the bag again, wishing it was my own body getting pummeled.

The pain is nothing less than I deserve for how I treated the girl I fucking adore.

"Timber. Timber!" Alaska avoids a flying fist as he gets in my face. "What's wrong with you? You've been beating the shit out of this thing for over an hour."

I swipe at the sweat on my face. "Move. It's none of your damn business." I sidestep him as I continue my workout.

"The hell it is. If there's something wrong—"

"There's not."

"Then you better figure whatever the hell it is out before you hurt yourself. Your body is shaking like a goddamn leaf right in front of me. Are you sleeping? Eating?"

I don't answer.

Of course, I haven't slept. That's the story of my life. My fuzzy brain tries to remember what I ate last. A bag of chips with whiskey yesterday?

"Shit... What happened with you and Lindy? Faith isn't talking, but I know something went down," he says.

"Leave it," I warn. Escaping his sharp perusal, I stomp away from Alaska without another word, unwrap my hands in the locker room, and grab my phone and wallet. Forget showering. I'm too wired to stay here any longer.

The sweat on my skin cools a little from the breeze outside, and I climb onto my bike before squealing out of the parking lot.

Alaska doesn't need to worry about me.

I'm fine.

CHAPTER SIXTEEN

LINDY

"What are you going to do?" Kat asks, uncharacteristically serious. It's book club night with the girls, and we're all huddled in Caroline's living room with spiked apple cider and a plethora of cozy blankets and pillows, a fire roaring in the stone fireplace.

Everyone knows about the sick episode at Rust, my subsequent rescue by Gideon, which then led to our date and my major freak-out. I've had days to contemplate my next move, plus a therapy session thrown in for good measure.

Sighing, I savor a sip of my cider before replying, "Apologize. Explain what was going on in my head."

"That's good," Faith says from her position across from me. "I'm not sure if you want to hear this, but Alaska said Timber isn't doing too well. He's been grinding too hard at the gym then overdrinking with the prospects, and you know he never loses control like that."

Caroline and Amelie nod in agreement. Both of them are familiar with Timber's usual demeanor because of how close their partners—Snow and Grim—are with their MC brother.

"Ugh, don't tell me that." I cover my face with a groan. "I feel bad enough already. He was so sweet and gentlemanly on our date. Really that's how he always acts. Then I screwed it all up by letting my past with Dean rear its ugly head."

"Hey, don't beat yourself up about it. You had a totally valid reaction, and Timber will understand. If he doesn't, then he's not the guy for you. He's not the man any of us think he is." Beth squeezes my arm.

Studying the five women who've become my closest friends this year, a wave of gratitude spills over. It was Dean and I for months after I isolated myself from the people around me. I wasn't sure I remembered how to make friends until I reached out to Caroline for help, and she invited me into her life—finding this cabin for me, introducing me to her book club friends.

Another wash of tears threatens to fall. "Gah!" I tip my head back and blink rapidly to ward them off. "You guys are going to make me cry again. Stop being so nice to me," I joke.

Kat grins, returning to her usual mischievous self. "Never. You're stuck with us, babe. Forever and ever, amen." She launches into the old country song and is quickly joined by the other women until laughter prevents another round of the chorus.

Feeling lighter than I have in a week, I set aside my nerves about talking to Gideon and focus on this—a group of strong, supportive women here for the long haul.

CHAPTER SEVENTEEN

LINDY

An opportunity to chat with Gideon arrives the next night when the club celebrates MC VP Fox's birthday and his work to solidify the deal with McCoy Security, a local firm who will handle the majority of the Reaper's Wolves security needs from now on.

Gideon is on the sidelines with a few club prospects, a beer in hand, and I swear I feel his eyes on me every so often, but whenever I check, he's focused on the conversation happening around him rather than me.

"No time like the present," Amelie says, staring pointedly at the man in question. Caroline and Faith follow her sightline and nod in encouragement.

Time to woman up.

Blowing out a hard exhale, I swallow the last of my water bottle—alcohol is off-limits for the time being considering what went down at Rust—and head toward the other side of the room. Rock music blares in the background as I weave through groups of Reaper's Wolves members, biker bunnies, and townie friends of each.

When Gideon is within hearing distance, my chin tips to the side, gesturing down the hall. "Can we talk in private for a minute?"

The wary expression on his face morphs into surprise, before he nods and follows me away from the loud party to an empty room dominated by a large conference table and chairs.

This must be where they hold club meetings.

"I'm sorry for how I reacted the other night," I blurt out the moment we're alone. No preamble. Straight to the point.

He jerks as if I tasered him with a volt of electricity. Maybe I did. It's obvious he expected something other than an apology.

"You don't have to apologize..."

"Yes, I do. It wasn't fair to freak out on you like that." I take a deep breath. Time to lay it on the line. "I could give you a lot of excuses for what happened. You're the first man I've been interested in since Dean. I didn't expect things to get hot and heavy so fast when that's never been my M.O. But it all boils down to being overwhelmed and not knowing how to handle the crash of emotions."

Timber shifts to take a step forward then stops himself, remaining stationed out of arm's reach. "Again, you don't have to apologize. Whatever the reason, it's valid. I never intended to push you too hard or too fast into something you didn't want. I can't tell you how much I regret—"

"No." I close the gap between us, and my fingertips cover his bottom lip. "No regrets. That's not what I'm saying. I've had a lot of time to think since that night. Long conversations with my therapist, too. And I'd like to try again, if that's okay. I totally understand if I've got too much baggage or—"

This time, Gideon is the one to stop me, his callused palm cupping my cheek. "I'm in. However you want me. However slow you need. *I'm in.* I've been in since that first day I saw you drive onto the compound—brave and beautiful."

"Yeah?" It's hard to believe he took one look at me, especially on a day where frazzled nerves were my norm, and thought I was beautiful or brave, but the truth is in his eyes.

And when he confirms it with a decisive nod then a hesitant kiss on my forehead, I melt into his strong arms, a little less worried about our future.

Maybe there's something behind that legend of *heart sparks*, after all.

OVER THE NEXT COUPLE of weeks, Gideon and I hang out almost everyday. Grabbing coffee at Crossing's Cups & Cakes. Splurging on games and Miss Patty's Rose Lemonades at Apple Fest. He even took me on the prettiest ride on his motorcycle through the mountains, where autumn colors reigned supreme.

True to his word, the physical aspect of our relationship moved at a glacial pace—never exceeding chaste hand holding and kisses on the cheek or forehead.

I have no right to be disappointed. It's exactly what I said I wanted.

But sexual frustration builds each time we're together and nothing happens.

Hypocrite, I chastise myself for being so fickle.

I can't freak out that first night then wish it would happen again so soon, but it's getting harder and harder to ignore my body's needs amongst all the talking and being near him ninety-percent of the time.

My cabin comes into view after a day at the zoo, and Gideon slows to a stop. "Don't forget your monkey!" He opens the black container attached to his motorcycle and removes the inflatable monkey he bought me.

"How could I forget Martin?" I laugh at his silliness. All I did was play with the little primate for a minute, and the next thing I knew, Gideon bought it for me.

The green monkey sits in one arm as I pull my purse over my shoulder, smiling at today's events. Our dates have focused on getting to know each other, despite being friends for a year already.

He told me about his life growing up with an uncle who sounds awful, and it hurts to know he suffered through that kind of abuse. I shared my family background and some more about Dean, which wasn't as difficult as I thought it'd be.

"I'll see you tomorrow?" Gideon asks as he walks me to the front door. I nod my head, accept an innocent kiss to my cheek, then wave goodbye before entering the cabin. He waits to make sure I'm safe inside—listening for the locks to engage—then straddles his bike and turns toward the clubhouse.

Damn, he looks good on that thing. All that hard muscle and gleaming metal creating a picture-perfect image for a *Hotties of the MC World* calendar.

That should definitely be a thing. I'd buy a dozen.

Imagining twelve months full of Gideon in various states of undress with his motorcycle as a prop, I drop my things off on the kitchen table. The refrigerator opens with a sticky crackling sound as I survey the options for dinner then deflate at the threadbare contents.

"Dammit," I mutter under my breath.

I was supposed to go grocery shopping yesterday but got caught up in the romance novel our club is reading. One about an uptight billionaire who becomes obsessed with his pregnant assistant.

Some readers might hate the pregnancy/baby tropes but not me. I fucking love to see a man take care of his woman and child—even if the kid may not be biologically his.

The clock on the stove shows that it's still early enough for the local grocery store to be open, so I reluctantly close the fridge and snag my purse, leaving Martin the Monkey behind.

CHAPTER EIGHTEEN

GIDEON

My phone rings, and Lindy's name pops up. Answering with a swipe of my thumb, I grin. "Hey, baby, how's it going?" We had a fun day at the zoo, so you'd think she had enough of me already, but I'm happy that's not the case. I can never get enough of my girl, especially after our rough start.

"I'm not sure."

There's tension in her voice, and immediately my shoulders stiffen. "What's wrong?"

"I think I'm being followed."

"What?" I straighten from my spot on the couch watching a college football game with Fox, Ranger, and Grim. Tiny's head is in my lap, but he senses the concern in my tone and sits up, a little whine coming from the back of his throat.

Someone mutes the television.

"I don't know if I'm being paranoid or what, but this car has been following me for the past fifteen minutes. It looks like an undercover cop vehicle with the bar of lights just under the top of the windshield. I can't tell if Dean's driving or one of his friends because of the tinted windows, but it's kind of freaking me out. I made a couple of random turns, and they followed each one, so now I'm worried they're going to pull me over."

"Don't panic. Stick to the speed limit. Use your turn signals, and get to the club as soon as you can. Even if they flash their lights, don't stop. How far away are you? Should I come and give you an escort?" I ask, hopping up from the couch.

"No, I'll be there soon," she says. Her breathing is heavy, her voice strained. "This could all be in my head. Just a weird coincidence."

"Don't do that. Don't minimize your instincts. Even if this is a false alarm, it's good that you're keeping aware of your surroundings." I head outside with Tiny and Ranger trailing behind me as backup, and I attempt to keep her calm by praising her survival instincts, but I'm not sure how well it works.

Eventually, her SUV rolls up to the clubhouse.

Sure enough, a black Charger bypasses the gravel drive a few minutes later. I can't see through the windows, but there's no doubt in my mind whoever's driving has something to do with Dean. Call it a gut feeling, but after years in the military, I learned early on to never ignore those.

"You okay?" I ask once Lindy gets out of the car.

"Yeah, I'm better now." She kneels to pet Tiny behind the ears, and he happily licks her face, generous with his slobbery kisses. "I'm glad they didn't follow me here, but why follow me at all?"

"I don't know." Though the bastard must have forgotten the dirt we have on him. The shady shit he doesn't want anyone to know about after we did some digging back when he was harassing Caroline to get to Lindy. "And it doesn't matter. He'll have to go through the entire club to get to you."

"I hate causing so much trouble."

"Hell no," I growl. "This isn't your fault. You're my Lindy Girl, and I protect what's mine. Do you want to pack a bag and stay with me at the clubhouse?"

"No, I think I'll be okay now that he's gone. If you could follow me home to double check no one's waiting around the corner or anything. I know it's paranoid but—"

"It's smart." I hate leaving her alone, though. So when Lindy and I arrive at her cabin five minutes later, I decide that I'm not.

"Thanks again... What are you doing?" she asks as I settle on her sofa after helping her put away the groceries she picked up.

"Spending the night. You're not staying by yourself."

"Gideon, you don't have to do that."

"Yes, I do. I can sleep on the couch if you want. I don't care, but I'm not leaving."

She sighs but nods, a look of relief flashing across her face before she turns to preheat the oven. "Okay. And you can sleep in the bed. We're both adults."

Damn right.

I vow to keep things strictly platonic tonight, despite having Lindy's warm curves so close.

I'm not going to fuck this up again.

CHAPTER NINETEEN

LINDY

We're both adults.

Famous last words that come back to bite me in the ass as I wiggle beneath the comforter next to Gideon. Sneaking a peek at my phone, I squint from the bright light and stifle a groan.

12:07 A.M.

It's barely after midnight?

Gideon and I went to bed a little over an hour ago, and I'm regretting the paranoia that had me dialing his number when I thought someone was tailing me. Because if I hadn't called him, I'd be asleep already. Probably. Maybe.

Okay, so my sleep isn't that great even without a giant man who smells like pine and oil creating a dip in the mattress, tempting me to roll into the divot and right into his arms.

That would totally demolish my 'take it slow' boundary.

You've known the man for over a year.

You've dated him for over a month.

How much slower do you need?

And let's not forget my hormones which riot for attention the moment he's in the vicinity. But what can I do? Accost the poor man in his sleep?

His breathing evened out soon after his head hit the pillow. Gideon's off in dreamland while I'm stuck in reality—hot, horny, and mad about it. My focus shouldn't be on testing the firmness of those broad shoulders and ridged abdomen. It should be on the weirdness from earlier.

On whether Dean or one of his cronies was following me home from the grocery store. But that asshole's taken up so much of my brainspace that I really don't want to think about him now, especially when fear for my safety is the last thing on my mind.

Honestly, I'm probably the safest I've been since the last time Gideon and I slept together—him on top of me like a guardian blanket.

"Ugh..." I sigh under my breath, flipping over to my right side.

"Care to share what's got you so frustrated?" Gideon's scratchy voice emanating through the dark sends me jerking back so fast I almost roll off the bed, until his muscular arm snags my waist and saves me from the abyss.

"You're awake?"

"I never fell asleep," he admits. "Hard to do next to a gorgeous woman. Who also prefers fidgeting every few seconds rather than resting."

"Sorry."

His other arm rests under his head as he stares at me through the dark. Moonlight offers a muted glow to the room but not enough to expunge the shadows. All I can make out is the gleam of his eyes and the flash of white teeth when he speaks.

"Want to talk about it, whatever's keeping you up? Is it Dean?"

"No, definitely not." I shift a little further away, praying the shadows hide my embarrassment.

"No, you don't want to talk about it, or no, it isn't your ex?" he asks, and the smirk on his face is almost palpable despite the lack of light.

Reaching beneath the covers, my fingers find the elastic waistband of his sweatpants and snap it against his stomach in retaliation for laughing at my flustered vagueness.

"Careful... You're playing with fire." The switch from playful teasing to growly alpha is intoxicating, so I snap the waistband again, my heartrate picking up in anticipation.

A rumble of thunder rolls through his body, vibrating from his lower stomach to my palm—something I pressed flat to his hot skin rather than removing it after taunting him.

"Is that a question, Lindy Girl? Because my answer is yes."

Swallowing past the thickness of my tongue, I whisper, "Good, because I don't want to go slow anymore," then inch my hand below the gray cotton until his dick springs free.

Pre-cum leaks from the mushroom head, and a hum of apprehension runs below my skin. Like the rest of Gideon's bulky stature, his cock matches—thick and long and oh-so-tempting. Nervous energy rides the coattails of arousal, my body getting turned on just from looking at him.

"You set the pace, baby, remember that," Gideon reminds me.

Nodding absentmindedly—my attention fixed on the huge dick in front of me—I rest my hands on his heavy thighs. "I'm not very good at this, so if you don't like something, tell me."

A quiet huff of laughter fills the air. "Trust me, whatever you decide to do, I'll enjoy it. Guaranteed."

What a different response compared to Dean. He'd made it no secret how disappointed he was in our sex life. *Stop thinking about that asshole!*

Taking Gideon's word for it, I lean forward and lick the prominent vein running under his cock in one long stroke. He bobs with the motion, so I wrap my hand around the wide base to hold him steady before lowering my head again to repeat the action.

The fat tip stretches my mouth as my lips purse around him like I'm sucking a popsicle.

Gideon's attention is focused on my mouth when I dare a glance upward, but his hands clutch the bedsheet in a tight grip while gravelly sounds of pleasure accompany each swipe of my tongue. Encouraged, I lick and suck, falling into a rhythm, as one hand tentatively slides lower to cup his balls. Another spurt of his salty flavor invades my mouth, but it isn't unpleasant.

Sliding further down, I take him deeper until he hits the back of my throat, and tears spring to my eyes. The position is uncomfortable yet empowering. Breathing through my nose, I force a swallow, the tense muscles undulating along his thick length.

"Damn, Lindy Girl. Such a pretty girl choking on my dick." Gideon's hand moves to clench my hair. So far, he hasn't been demanding, but as his control disintegrates, the more his hand guides me up and down.

Something I don't mind in the least.

I like his firm grip showing me what he wants.

I desperately want to please him.

Our speed increases and Gideon grunts. "I'm about to blow, baby. Get off unless you want me to fill your belly with cum."

My eyes find his, and he must see my approval because after a few jerky thrusts into my mouth, his cock swells then his hot seed hits my tongue. I swallow as much as I can, although some escapes down the edges of my mouth. Sucking gently on the tip, I draw out the last of his release before giving a goodbye lick and raising his sweatpants to cover him again.

My fingers swipe his cum from my lips, and I suck it off my fingers as Gideon watches with hooded eyes.

"Where the fuck did you learn that?" Gideon shakes his head in disbelief then lifts to his elbows to pull me in for a hard kiss. "You're gonna be the death of me, but I'll die a very happy man."

I flush at his praise. It feels good knowing I have the power to destroy his control. To bring him intense pleasure. Especially since he holds the same power over me—our first date evidence of that.

Cuddling next to him, I tease, "Hopefully, you'll live a very long, very happy life before then." I cover a yawn, sleepy after the adrenaline abandons me. Who knew sucking a man off could be so calming? *Ish.* There's still a simmering heat between my thighs, but I don't have the energy to do much about it.

Sleep or orgasm?

The struggle is real.

"Oh, I plan on it." Gideon's palm sweeps down my side as his head dips to press a kiss to my neck. "In fact, I'm going to continue living that happy life by eating out my sweet girl. Think you can handle that, baby?"

My eyes close as I arch my hips in invitation.

Guess a girl *can* have it all...

CHAPTER TWENTY

GIDEON

Lindy's silent consent is all I need to slide beneath the comforter and divest her of the purple cotton panties blocking my view of her pussy. I've dreamed of tasting her sweet cunt for months now, and after that small taste I had on her porch weeks ago, it's become a feral need.

"God, you smell good," I mutter, inhaling the scent of her arousal. Lindy moans and rocks her hips again, and I don't plan on making my girl wait any longer.

Burying my face between her pale thighs, I spread her legs wider as my tongue laps at the glossy wetness coating her folds from clit to slit. My girl made a fucking mess of herself while sucking me off, and it has my dick rallying for a second round.

She'd swallowed me whole like in all of my dreams, except reality had been much better. Her initial adorable hesitancy. Then her eagerness to please.

I've never had someone so intent on getting me off.

Women usually went down on me or gave me a hand job because they wanted something. An in with the club. Bragging rights with their friends.

No one has ever pleasured me with no expectations of something in return—except Lindy. She'd snuggled into my side the moment she'd drained the last of my release from me.

No leading comments. No straddling my hips or face to force reciprocation.

Not that I would have minded.

But Lindy got comfortable, yawned, and looked ready to fall asleep, rather than expecting me to even the score. Which made me that much more motivated to send her off to a good night's sleep with a mindblowing orgasm.

Lindy's breath hitches in her chest as I flick her swollen clit with my tongue, then exhales as I suckle the sweet bud. She's in that soft space between dreams and reality, and I'm happy to keep her floating for as long as possible.

Twisting my head, I nibble on the sensitive inner lips of her pussy before rimming her tight channel with the tip of my tongue, plunging forward a second later. Immediately, her walls flutter around the pliant muscle, and I wish I could give her something thicker to hold on to, but this will have to do for now.

I'm not trying to work her up into a frenzy.

I'm focused on seducing a bone-melting release from her lax body.

"Mmm..."

"That's my line, Lindy Girl." I hum in satisfaction, allowing the vibrations to slide along her soaking cunt. "You taste so good. Like you were made just for me."

She shudders, another gush of arousal spilling onto my tongue, and I lap it up like the sweet treasure it is. I lose track of time, lost in the warm cocoon of her plump thighs around my ears, her curves overflowing my palms on her hips.

There's just Lindy—breathy sighs, purrs of contentment.

And me—devouring my beautiful woman, ensuring her dreams are soft and nightmare-free like she deserves.

CHAPTER TWENTY-ONE

LINDY

The next day comes too soon. After Gideon spent—minutes, hours?—with his bearded face buried in my pussy, waking up is a major letdown, even if my phone's clock says it's technically the afternoon.

I haven't slept so well in ages.

But the sun peering through the window refuses to let me return to blissful dreams of Gideon, so I roll to my side with a groan.

"Hey, sleepyhead. You're finally awake." Gideon readjusts the arm wrapped around my waist.

"Mhmm... Someone put me in an orgasm-induced coma last night," I joke.

"Sounds intense." He strokes my wild hair, the curls a tangly mess. "But you're okay? No regrets?"

"Not one," I say honestly. My stomach grumbles, voicing its distress after missing breakfast. "Except for skipping a meal, apparently. Want some lunch?"

"Sure, what are you craving? I can whip something up."

Hopping out of bed, I stretch my arms toward the ceiling, enjoying the way Gideon's eyes drop appreciatively from my face, breasts, and pussy before moving up again. "Don't worry, I've got this. You relax while I get things going."

"You cooked for me last time. I don't expect—"

"Cooking is my love language." Bending over, I kiss his cheek like he usually does to me then traipse out of the room toward the kitchen after snagging an oversized sleepshirt.

It's been awhile since I've regularly cooked for another person. I forgot how much it meant to me to be able to care for someone in such a simple way.

Something else Dean ruined with his snide remarks.

This chicken is too salty.

You should have let this bake longer.

Feeling an itch of uneasiness despite the earlier peace, I boil a pot of water before stirring in the noodles for macaroni and cheese. Comfort food is exactly what I need right now.

As I stand over the stove, two strong arms wrap around me from behind, and I freeze, even though I recognize Gideon's presence.

"It's just me." He nuzzles the side of my neck and squeezes me a little tighter to him.

"I know." A forced sham of a laugh bubbles out. "You startled me." I turn my head to see him better. His eyes are bright, and the corners of his mouth twitch as if he's holding back a smile.

He's happy.

And I love seeing that. Knowing I'm the cause of it.

But there's still that uncomfortable itch.

Searing pain.

With a shout of surprise, I rip my hand back from the overflowing pot in front of me. Hot water splashes over the sides, and Gideon quickly twists the dial to lower the heat and grabs my hand.

I shiver at the gentle touch but let him lead me to the sink where he runs water over the burn. The sting abates a little but returns once I remove my hand.

"Damn, I shouldn't have distracted you," he says. "Keep your hand here. I'll check to see if you have something for burns."

"Medicine cabinet in the bathroom."

"Okay. I'll be right back." Two minutes later, Gideon strides into the kitchen with a bottle of aloe vera meant for sunburns. After drying my hand with a dishtowel, he rubs the gel on the back of my hand. The wound isn't very big, but it hurts like hell. "Is that better? Lindy?"

His voice sounds muted. Another shiver skitters down my spine. Why am I cold? That doesn't make sense.

"Lindy? What's wrong?" He reaches for my cheek, and I involuntarily flinch in my seat at the dining table.

Oh, god. What was that? Gideon wasn't going to hurt me. He'd never hurt me.

Logically, I know that's true. But my body isn't running on logic right now. Between the reminder of Dean's insults and the blast of pain from my cooking, they triggered a trauma response—something I don't want Gideon to see. It's not his fault, and I don't want him shouldering the blame for my brain's issues.

"Lindy?"

Swallowing the icepicks in my throat, I manage a few words. "I need a minute, please."

"Do you want me to go?"

Inhale. Exhale. Slow, even breaths. Licking my lips, I shake my head. "No, you don't need to leave. I just need time and space to calm down."

Gideon nods, concern a heavy mask on his face. "Okay, baby."

He grabs the wooden spoon I was using and stirs the macaroni, watching the noodles until they're done. Straining them at the sink, he mixes the final ingredients in then fills two bowls, setting them on the table.

"Thank you," I murmur, feeling marginally better.

I like that Gideon wants to take care of me. By being my guardian shadow. By making me lunch. By respecting my boundaries, listening to what I need and abiding by it.

"Does anything ever rocket you back to your past with your uncle?"

Understanding washes over his worried expression. "Cans of Michelob. It was his drink of choice."

My chin dips in acknowledgment. "Dean always had something to say at every meal. At first, I was open to suggestions, but then it became obvious that nothing I did would please him."

"He's an asshole."

I fork a bite of mac and cheese into my mouth. "True. I'm sorry I flinched earlier. That wasn't about you." I slide my hand across the table in a peace offering, which Gideon promptly accepts.

"Thank you for explaining, but you don't have to apologize. Just continue to let me know what you need, and we'll be good, okay?"

Breathing easier for the first time in the last hour, I consciously lower my hunched shoulders and sit straighter.

"Okay."

He smooths his thumb over my uninjured hand, and we sit quietly eating the rest of our lunches, before Gideon voices a question.

"Why aren't you afraid of me? Of any of the MC members?"

It's a fair question and one I've asked myself numerous times. Dean was an abusive asshole and law enforcement. The Reaper's Wolves guys are all ex-military, so on the surface, there's not much difference between them.

They are men familiar with violence.

Yet, I've never truly felt fear on the compound.

Maybe it's because Caroline vouched for the guys. Maybe Dean was so bad that I didn't have any fear left over to worry about the Reaper's Wolves.

"Lindy?"

"Sorry... I'm still processing my thoughts," I say then shrug. "Honestly, there are several reasons why, but the main one is compartmentalization. Dean is one man who hurt me. He's in a very specific box. When I look at you or Snow or any of the other guys, there's a distinction. You're not in the box."

I think I hear him mutter 'Thank fuck' under his breath, and his palpable relief makes me smile.

Gideon has never been in the same category as Dean.

He's got his own very special category in my heart.

CHAPTER TWENTY-TWO

GIDEON

I invited Lindy to hang out at the gym with me a few days after our talk over mac and cheese, figuring we could both use the physical release of jumping rope or punching a bag. I hate that she struggles with triggers still, but I get it, and my chest warms at the trust she showed by allowing me to stay and discuss what happened.

Lindy arrives while I'm in the middle of sparring with Denver—a man on his way up the MMA chain. It won't be long before he hits it big. Hopefully, spotlighting the gym with him.

I wave Lindy over to a row of chairs along the wall as I finish up.

"Alright, that's enough," Alaska calls out. Denver and I walk to our corners and gulp long drinks of water before he joins me and gestures to Lindy with his bottle.

"Is she your girl?"

"Hell yeah, so don't get any ideas." I eye him in part warning, part joking. I don't think he'd try anything, but it's always good to let another man know where you stand when it comes to your woman.

"Point taken," he chuckles. "I just meant that she kind of stands out. Doesn't look like the usual club bunnies that hang out here and the clubhouse."

I glance at Lindy. One leg is crossed over the other as she hunches over a crossword puzzle in her lap. She started doing them a few weeks back after lamenting the state of her memory.

If she wasn't wearing tight yoga pants and a neon-colored tank, she would fit right in with the people at the senior center down the block. "That's because she's not, but for some reason, she's chosen me anyway."

"I guess that makes you a lucky son of a bitch," Denver jokes.

"Damn straight. See you later, man." We bump fists then I head Lindy's way. "Hey, baby."

She smiles up at me as she puts her puzzle away. *Damn.* I never want her to stop looking at me like that. Like I'm her favorite person in the world.

"Are you going to show me some moves now?" She playfully throws up her fists in a mock fighting stance, and I chuckle at her antics as I grab her bag.

"First, let's lock this up so no one messes with it, then I'll show you my moves." I lower my voice suggestively.

Lindy blushes but plays along. "Hmm, sounds interesting... But I warn you, my boyfriend's a behemoth, and I'm not sure he'd like you flirting with me."

Fuck, I like the sound of her calling me her boyfriend. It's a paltry word in comparison to my feelings for Lindy, but I'll take whatever she wants to call me. "No, ma'am. This is completely professional." I wink.

After we return to the main gym area, I tape her knuckles.

"Now, I really look badass."

What she looks like is fucking sexy. Like she plays rough before fucking the life out of you. *Shit. Erase that image.* I don't need the whole gym to see my damn hard-on. Hiding behind a punching bag, I steady it for Lindy.

"Let me see what you got."

She slams her fist into the bag, barely moving it. "Damn, that's hard!"

"Put more weight behind your punches. Try again."

We work our way through the gym with me showing her proper techniques and teaching some self-protective measures. God forbid Lindy is ever alone with Dean or some other abusive bastard, but I want her prepared in case I'm not around.

"Let's take a break," I say an hour later.

Lindy is breathing hard, unaccustomed to this kind of exertion. Shooting me a grateful look, she sits down on the edge of the empty boxing ring, gulps her water, and lays back with her arms splayed above her head.

"You know as much as Alaska and his staff try to keep this place clean, this thing's been covered with sweat, blood, and who knows what else."

"Don't care." Lindy doesn't bother to lift her head to respond.

I shake my head in amusement and join her on the mat. My girl is worn out.

She warned me when I first asked her to come that she's passed out from working out too hard in the past. Twice. So, I tried to keep things easy. I wanted to push her limits, not harm her.

"Are you okay? Do you feel like you're going to pass out?"

"I'm fine. If we'd kept going, something might have happened since I was beginning to feel dizzy, but I'm good now."

Frustration winds through my body. "You were 'beginning to feel dizzy'? Why didn't you tell me? If I push too hard, you need to let me know."

Lindy sighs, and I can practically hear the roll of her eyes behind her closed eyelids. "I'm fine, Gideon. We stopped. The dizziness is fading. Relax."

"Lindy, if your safety is compromised then I need to know. There's a fine line between brave and foolish." She ignores me, probably too tired to argue, so I let it go, but make a mental note to pay better attention in the future. Now that I'm aware of her baseline and limit, I can adjust.

"Why is it so quiet all of a sudden?" she asks.

"The gym closes for an hour around this time. Most guys go home to eat then come back later."

Alaska tries to accommodate every type of schedule, so the gym opens at five in the morning and closes at midnight.

"You're saying we're alone then." Lindy sits up with a mischievous twinkle in her eyes. "Good, because I've wanted to do this since I walked in and saw you all sweaty and hot sparring with that guy." She moves to hover above my face then kisses me.

Instinctively, I tug her leg over, so she's straddling me, and run my free hand under her loose tank, enjoying the feel of her squishy belly before I move higher. A slight gasp escapes when my fingers feel under the sports bra for her nipple.

I wonder if she's going to stop me from going further, but Lindy presses harder into me as our kiss intensifies. The heat of her cunt a torturous temptation on my dick.

Little wisps of curls escape her ponytail, tickling my face and catching on my beard the longer we make out. They tease with their featherlight touches, and I imagine those caresses tickling over my entire body.

She rubs her entire front along mine as her hands curl into my shoulder and scalp. The small pain from her little fingernails digging into me is hot as fuck.

I want Lindy's marks.

I'm hers, and I don't care who knows it.

A throat clears in the background, and I whip Lindy underneath me so fast, her dazed look of confusion almost makes me grin.

My head lifts to see who the intruder is. No one deserves to see Lindy in a state of arousal. She's mine. For my eyes only.

Fucking Ranger.

"Sorry, guys. Alaska said Timber was here, and when you didn't answer your phone..." He shrugs and scratches the back of his neck. "We've got an issue at Reaper's Revamp. A client claims you fucked up his bike and won't calm down until he talks to you."

"Dammit," I mutter. Maneuvering to a standing position, I help Lindy up then face Ranger. "I'll be there in ten minutes. Make sure you have the paperwork for the job ready for me when I arrive, because the guy's lying. I didn't fuck up anyone's ride."

"You got it. Sorry again." Ranger waves farewell then exits the gym, leaving Lindy and I alone again.

Too bad we can't finish what we started.

"Sounds like you've got a fire to put out, which is for the best since I should stop playing hooky to work, too," Lindy says, patting my chest. "The macro I left running is probably done now, so I should get home anyway. But this," she gestures between us, her hardened nipples and my erect cock on display beneath our clothes, "To be continued."

THIS PRICK IS OUT OF his damn mind. The paperwork clearly states what he ordered and what we delivered. Pictures of before and after included.

Yet he has the nerve to argue I'm wrong.

"I'm going to sue this place for everything you've got," he threatens.

"Go ahead. It's your money you'll be wasting because the law is on our side." I cross my arms over my chest. Usually my size does the trick of intimidating people but this guy is so far gone, common sense and self-preservation have clearly deserted him.

A notification dings on my phone, interrupting the standoff. Swiping to open it, my brows furrow at the message. It's an alert from McCoy Security about a breach on the south side of the MC compound.

It's a forest of trees on that side of the property. Did a deer or bear trigger the alarm? Surely, McCoy accounts for forest creatures.

"We're done here," I say, a niggling worry creeping up my back. The man splutters, but he's soon forgotten once the roar of my Harley fills my ears.

I'm not the only club member who would have gotten that alert. Snow and Fox would have, too. In the MC's hierarchy, we're the top three men—Club President, VP, and Sergeant at Arms.

Texting Snow and Fox that I'm headed back to the clubhouse, I rev the engine and peel out of the Reaper's Revamp parking lot, uneasiness my companion.

CHAPTER TWENTY-THREE

LINDY

Goosebumps pop up over my skin as soon as I step into my darkened living room. The fall chill from outside has me viciously rubbing my bare arms to ward off the cold.

I should have worn a jacket over my tank top, but I figured I'd be in and out of the weather too quickly to need one. Besides, when I left the gym, my body was too hot from grinding all over Gideon's muscular body to need an extra layer.

I can't wait to pick up where we left off.

Smiling at the prospect, I enter the kitchen and pause. There's another bouquet of yellow daisies on the counter.

Would someone from the club let themselves into my home to drop them off?

That doesn't make sense since last time they left them on the porch mat.

I take one wary step forward when a hand covers my mouth and somebody slams me into the wall.

"You thought you could escape me so easily? You'll always be mine." The familiar voice of Dean rumbles in my ear and fear shoots down my spine.

Twisting, I try to gain enough purchase to injure him, but he tosses me into a kitchen chair first, then stalks forward.

In my head I'm screaming for help, letting someone know there's trouble. But my throat closes up. It's like my mouth is stuffed with cotton balls and nothing wants to come out.

"Think again, bitch. You're gonna pay for leaving me. And then you're gonna pay some more for letting that bastard fuck what's mine." Dean backhands me, and the spot throbs under the powerful force of his hand.

Whimpering, I cover the bruised cheek and stumble to my feet, forcing words past my tightening throat. "You need to leave before I call the cops."

He laughs—an evil, dark thing.

"The cops? Bitch, I *am* the cops. Who do you think is gonna help you?" He slaps my other cheek, whipping my head around and causing me to lunge into the table. Glass shatters as an empty tumbler crashes to the floor.

"You think your buddies can protect you from assaulting a woman in her own home? This is trespassing. Have you forgotten we're not in Everton? You have no authority here."

"I have all the authority, slut!" he shouts. "After your friend sicced her biker boyfriend on me, I wondered if they were harboring you. Then I saw you with that huge motherfucker at the Club Wolf fire, and I knew for sure. You're fucking him, aren't you?"

Ducking beneath the table, my hands skim the floor, searching for anything to use as a weapon, when I find a shard of broken glass. Wrapping it in my hand, I swallow the hiss of pain as it slices my palm.

Fight back, Lindy.

You don't have to take his bullshit anymore.

Levering to my feet, I swing around and plunge it into the first body part I reach. His arm. Dean yells in pain, blood streaking his forearm, and I race toward the front door, managing to rip it open before his hand catches my shirt.

We tumble onto the front porch and down the steps until we lay in a heap on the ground outside.

"You fucking cunt!" *Slap.* "You think you're stronger than me?" *Slap.* "Think you can beat me?"

Consciousness fades in and out as blood fills my mouth. My fingers scratch at his face as I try to gather enough force to roll him off me, but he's too heavy. And all he does is keep screaming in my face.

"You got lucky at Rust. I told Martha to..."

Martha? She's working with Dean? That would explain why I got sick. Why I haven't heard from her since that night.

Slap.

I almost laugh at his technique. Slaps, really? The most demeaning way to hurt someone.

I hate that the someone is me.

Clawing at his face, neck, anywhere I can reach, I try fighting him off, blocking a few swings of his arm.

Suddenly, the roar of a steel calvary pierces the fog surrounding me. Growls and shouts emanate in the air as the weight is lifted from my chest. Familiar men clothed in leather kneel around me, but I don't see the one I want through my swollen eye sockets.

Fox helps me to a sitting position, and that's when Dean and Gideon come into focus. Gideon is wailing on Dean with his fists, and I can't help a smirk.

Serves him right.

Violence in any form should frighten me, but it's obvious verbal threats don't matter to Dean or else he would have heeded Snow's warning from months ago. Instead, he broke into my cabin.

A physical beatdown is fucking justice in my mind.

"You should stop Gideon before he kills him." That's what I want to say, but I'm not sure if that's what comes out of my mouth because it's painful to talk.

Someone must understand though, or have the same thought, because Snow and Fox pull Gideon off Dean.

A cop car arrives with lights flashing, and I'm afraid it's one of Dean's friends here to arrest us, until Sheriff Lawson gets out and cuffs my ex.

An ambulance parks beside the cop car, and the EMTs split, one approaching me while the other goes to Dean.

Then the rest of the evening is a blur. Doctors and nurses poking and prodding. Caroline and Faith crying in the corner of my hospital room, being comforted by their men.

Throughout it all, Gideon is a constant by my side.

My face is sore as hell, I have a concussion from being knocked about, and stitches for the cut on my hand, but things could be worse.

Broken bones.

Dead.

"Are you up to talking with PD? An officer is waiting in the hall to get your statement," Gideon says, stroking my arm above the IV in my hand.

"Send them in. Might as well get it over with."

A Suitor's Crossing deputy enters the room as everyone but Gideon files out, and once his pen's poised above his little notebook, I relay what happened, including Dean's mention of Martha.

"You think she drugged you?" the deputy asks.

"I can't say for sure. Maybe my sickness really was a random stomach bug, but either way, it's odd. I'm not even sure how Dean and Martha know each other. They might have met once at a company party we attended as a couple...?" I shrug my shoulders, too tired to figure out how my former coworker fits into all of this.

"We'll certainly look into it, ma'am. Is there anything else we should know?"

Gideon pins the deputy with a hard stare. "Did your department receive the file on Dean's illegal actions while on duty in Everton?"

"Yes, Sheriff Lawson thanks the Reaper's Wolves for the information." The officer closes his notebook and clips the pen to his shirt pocket. "If that's all, I'll see myself out. If we have any more questions, we'll be in touch. Take care now."

Once Gideon and I are alone, I settle into the lumpy hospital pillow and turn my head to face him. "Did the doctor say how long I'd have to stay? We can monitor the concussion at home."

"They want to keep you for a 24-hour observation period. Just relax and rest. Enjoy the pain meds." His finger gently feathers down one swollen cheek.

Sighing, I close my eyes. "Damn Dean. This is the first time he actually put me in the hospital."

"It will be the last time, too," Gideon promises. "I'm sorry I wasn't there sooner. Snow, Fox, and I got the alert of a security breach, but they went to check the southern property border while I was coming from Reaper's Revamp. McCoy Security didn't have cameras set up yet, so the guys had to manually track the intruder to your cabin."

"Well, even if they'd failed tracking school, I'm sure the ruckus Dean and I caused once outside would've drawn attention from the clubhouse. I should have aimed for his neck with that glass shard," I mutter. Although having Dean's death on my hands would suck—it'd ensure he haunted me forever when I want to forget about his existence.

"You still got him, though. I saw the gash. It was long and deep."

"A lot of good it did me." A brow raises as I point to my puffy face. I feel like an overfilled balloon about to burst.

"You slowed him down. That counts for a lot when seconds matter. How are you feeling otherwise?"

The rhythmic beep of the heart monitor sounds in the background as I take stock of my mind and body. The adrenaline is gone, leaving a massive hangover. Physically, I'm weary and wounded, but emotionally?

Months ago, an altercation with Dean would have sent me spiraling into fear—triggering a fight or flight response—but aside from remnants of my earlier terror, I feel mostly fine. Victorious, even.

I fought back rather than letting fear immobilize me, and Dean is behind bars. It's possible he might get out on bail, but I don't think he's going to be able to weasel out of assault charges, breaking and entering, plus whatever dirt the MC dug up on him. He's getting locked away for good.

"Surprisingly okay," I admit, finally answering Gideon's question. Grabbing his hand, I bring it to my chest, right over my heart. "Dean doesn't have power over me any longer. He hasn't in a while, but today really helped it sink in. I'm not the same person I was when we were together. I've grown and become a stronger, more resilient version of myself. Thanks to therapy, the book club girls, and you."

"Don't give me too much credit. You were already strong as fuck when we met—getting away from Dean, trusting the MC, a bunch of strangers I might add, to protect you. I only played a small part in everything."

"No, you didn't. But I'll let you stay humble," I tease before covering a yawn. "Think you can fit in this bed with me? I wouldn't mind a warmer blanket." The one currently settled over my legs and belly isn't doing much to combat the icy air conditioning blowing overhead.

"I doubt it, but I'm willing to try." He carefully moves the IV line and cords out of the way then balances on the edge of the thin mattress. His heavy weight alleviates the last bit of stress bearing down on me as he gingerly spoons my back.

"You're the best comforter," I mumble, snuggling into his solid warmth.

"You're the best. Period, Lindy Girl. Now get some sleep. I'm not going anywhere."

CHAPTER TWENTY-FOUR

TWO WEEKS LATER

GIDEON

Cryptic flower bouquets and notes.

Hooking up with Martha to snare the gullible woman into a plan of drugging then kidnapping Lindy if I hadn't been at Rust.

Having his buddy tail Lindy's SUV.

Hiking through the woods behind the Reaper's Wolves MC compound to sneak into her cabin.

Dean is a certifiable psychopath. Which came as no surprise to me, but he'd held it together for a long time before tipping over the edge.

Seeing us at Club Wolf was the straw that broke the camel's back—he couldn't stand the thought of her with anyone else, even if Lindy and I weren't officially dating yet.

Thankfully, my girl will never have to see the bastard again because he's locked up tight in a federal prison.

The FBI swooped in upon his arrest—including Ranger, who apparently was an undercover agent sussing out our club while also working on a case of law enforcement corruption. Ranger and his FBI friends had been trailing Dean's group for a while, and his screw-up by attacking Lindy delivered him right to them.

It looks like he'll get some safety precautions—cops don't do well in prison—for spilling details about the dirty men higher up the food chain, but he's not getting off scot-free.

"Hey, why the broody face? You're not thinking about Dean again, are you?" Lindy skips into Reaper's Revamp. An aura of happiness surrounds her these days, and I'm proud to be a part of that.

The shop closed an hour ago, so it's just me left tinkering around on a custom order, while Lindy enjoyed book club. Except she's here instead of with her girls.

Wiping my hands on a stained rag, I welcome her hug and drop a kiss to her forehead. "My mind was wandering. What are you doing here? Tonight's your girls' night."

Lindy grins and plays with the zipper of my coveralls. "I ditched them since we've got some unfinished business."

"Is that so?"

The glide of the zipper lowering is barely audible above our breathing, and I relish the cool breeze filtering through my undershirt. Inch by inch, the coveralls slowly loosen until I can shrug the upper portion off my shoulders and arms. An elastic waist keeps the pants stationary as the sturdy fabric falls back.

"Remember how at the gym I said *to be continued*?" Lindy licks her lips and steps back with a sly twinkle in her eyes.

Losing her jacket, she turns her back to me and braces her hands on the metal tool counter behind us, bending in half to wiggle her juicy ass in my face as I finally notice the extremely short skirt she's wearing. It does nothing to cover the bare cheeks suddenly staring at me.

"Where the hell did you find this get-up?" The leather skirt is paired with a skin-tight tee and knee-high socks, and the realization that the back of her shirt says 'Property of Timber' has my cock threatening to rip through the coveralls.

"In the sale aisle. I was searching for discounted Halloween candy and found this costume instead. Do you like it?" She shakes her ass again then has the audacity to raise the back of the skirt higher as her body sinks into a deeper arch so her glistening pussy is in full view.

"I fucking love it." Crashing to my knees, I ignore the pain of the concrete on my bones and shove my face between those full cheeks, licking a path straight to her wet cunt.

Despite progressing by leaps and bounds before her attack, we've taken things slow the past two weeks.

I've been waiting for Lindy to initiate things, and damn, is this worth waiting for.

CHAPTER TWENTY-FIVE

LINDY

When I bought the sexy bounty hunter costume, I imagined Gideon and I cruising through the mountains—a man and his woman outfitted in leather—which made it a no-brainer purchase. After using Beth's craft supplies to add the 'Property of Timber' bit, and yes, my friends teased me mercilessly for that, I couldn't wait any longer to show it off.

Gideon's reaction is more than I hoped for.

We've been tiptoeing around sex since Dean's assault, but I'm healed and eager to jump my man's H.OT. *hot* body.

Dean who?

My thoughts are all about the strong, silent biker with a military past and family trauma to boot. A man who hasn't let life chip away at his kindness. A man whose sex appeal comes from more than rock hard abs and broad shoulders, but from the respect and care he shows me.

"Oh, fuck..." I moan as his lips clamp around my clit and suck.

A quick swat to my ass follows as he playfully reprimands me. "Language, baby."

"*Fuck* me, Gideon," I taunt, desperate for more than his talented tongue and fingers. Don't get me wrong, they're awesome, but the only thing that can satisfy me now is that big dick pounding into my pussy.

Damn, it's been too long since I've had sex. I'm horny as hell.

"Such a brat," he grunts before rising to his feet. He disappears for a moment, the loss of his heat sending a chill over my exposed body, but then he's back, his shadow eclipsing me as I feel his cock nudge my entrance.

"Is this what you want?" With one hard thrust, Gideon buries his full length deep, shoving me into the edge of the counter.

"Yes, yes, yes..." It becomes a coarse chant as he fucks me into the unforgiving metal. My breasts ache, smashed into an overflowing valley that threatens to suffocate me as I duck my head, pushing back into each of Gideon's savage thrusts.

He's not treating me like a piece of hand blown glass that can break with the slightest touch. It's sweet when his caresses are gentle and soothing, but I love when he loses control, too. And I plan to push him over the edge more often because the results are... *Chef's kiss. 10/10. No notes.*

"My filthy girl. Coming in here dressed like a—What are you supposed to be?"

"A sexy bounty hunter," I hiss, gasping at the direct drag of his cock along my G-spot.

"Mmm... Sexy bounty hunter. I'm going to fuck you over my bike in this outfit," he growls, his hand forcing itself between the counter and my chest to tweak a bruised nipple. "Then I'm going to get 'Property of Timber' put on all your clothes, so everyone knows you're mine."

Damn, who knew Gideon had such an insane possessive streak?

Good thing I'm a huge fan of dark romance...

"Does that mean you're getting 'Property of Lindy' on your stuff, too?"

He nips at my nick, biting his way to my earlobe. "That's getting tattooed over my heart, Lindy Girl. Now, is this sexy little pussy ready to come? I know you're hot for it. Hungry for my huge cock to stretch your tight cunt. Hungry for my cum to stuff you full." Gideon's crude words are like a lash along my clit, teasing me higher and higher.

"You're going to walk out of here dripping wet with your cream and my seed coating these pretty thighs. You're going to ride on the back of my Harley bare cunt to the leather seat, so you feel every rumble of the engine tempting you to come again. But you'll wait until we're home, won't you, baby?"

I can't respond.

Coherent thoughts are impossible.

All I can focus on is the burning pleasure ripping through my body as he hammers into me. As the lust and passion erupt in a rain of sparks so blinding I squeeze my eyes shut and scream with the climactic release.

"That's it. Scream. Cry. Wring this dick dry, baby." Gideon shudders and roars with the force of his orgasm, yet he still powers through it, pumping into me with jerky thrusts until we're both panting, collapsed on the tool counter.

"I love you, Lindy Girl," he whispers unexpectedly, and tears rise to the forefront.

This isn't post-coital chitchat. Gideon means what he says.

And he loves me.

Breathing deeply, I can't help the smile forming on my face pressed against the cool metal. Eventually, we'll have enough strength to stand up and go home, but for now, the only energy I need is to utter four words I never thought I'd say again.

"I love you, too."

EPILOGUE

GIDEON

The famous Suitor's Crossing bridge has a handful of tourists crossing its wooden planks, but that doesn't deter us. Lindy and I want to officially walk across the bridge together to cement our *heart spark* fate.

It's kind of kooky, and unnecessary considering nothing will change how I feel about her, but the rare sunny day in autumn means getting out into nature to revel in it, which is what we're doing.

"This is so cute," Lindy says, her bright green eyes absorbing the romantic atmosphere of twinkly lights, painted red accents, and couple names etched into the wood railings.

"Is this your first time at the bridge?"

"Yeah... I didn't want to tempt fate. I've walked the trails around here, though. You?"

"There wasn't any fear of tempting fate once I met you, so I've been here once or twice while exploring the area."

"Because you knew immediately I was your *heart spark*." She rolls her eyes like she doesn't believe me, but the twitch of a smile on her lips says the sentiment pleases her all the same.

We step around a couple stopped in the middle of the bridge for a selfie, continuing our ambling journey forward.

"Don't act like I was the only one who knew. I fielded a ton of shit from the guys for how far gone I was—*am*—for you."

"Caroline and the gang were the same with me. Freaking *heart spark* detectors," she jokes.

Once we reach the end of the bridge, she looks up at me with an impish expression. "Well? Do you still love me? Am I still your *heart spark*?"

"Damn straight." An older couple reprimands me for cursing, and Lindy giggles. Drawing her away from the crowd of people, I wrap her in my arms, relishing the privilege of holding her so close. There was a time I never thought this would happen. When I thought I fucked up so badly that Lindy would never let me near her again.

Thank fuck I was wrong.

Because I need my Lindy Girl—she's my heart and soul.

My brave little *heart spark*.

The Reaper's Wolves MC isn't done yet. VP Fox, undercover FBI Special Agent Ranger, and more have forthcoming stories!

THANKS FOR READING & DON'T FORGET TO RATE/ REVIEW!

Please consider leaving a rating/review. Ratings & reviews are the #1 way to support an indie author like me.
Also, don't miss out on free books and up-to-date release information. You can sign up for my newsletter here[1].
I appreciate your support!
XO, Hallie

---

1. https://www.thearrowedheart.com/hallie-bennett

ABOUT THE AUTHOR

Hallie prefers steamy, insta-love stories where curvy girls are claimed by filthy-talking heroes. And when she ran out of reading material, she decided to write her own stories. If you want a quick, hot read, she's your girl!